He co... ... Charlie bent his head and very gently brushed his mouth against hers. And Sor'... was starting to kiss him !

God, he wa...ed this so much. Wanted to feel her body close to his. Wanted her to kiss his demons away.

It couldn't happen. He had to stop.

Except he couldn't. Not when it felt so good, so right, to hold her and kiss her.

The beep of a car horn shocked them apart.

He dragged in a breath. 'I'm sorry. I shouldn't have done that. I just...' Just couldn't help himself. Wanted to be a real person, for once, instead of Charlie, Baron Radley. Wanted Sophie's warmth to enfold him.

'Don't worry. I won't be ringing *Celebrity Life* to give them a kiss-and-tell,' she said dryly.

He shook his head. 'That isn't what I meant. But we have to work together. I think it's best if we ignore what just happened.'

POSH DOCS
Honourable, eligible, and in demand!

Baron Rupert Charles Radley
The Hon. Sebastian Henry Radley
The Hon. Victoria Radley

Three aristocratic doctors, the very best in their field,
who just can't avoid the limelight!

In this exciting and emotional new trilogy from
bestselling author **Kate Hardy** read how these eligible
medics do their best to stay single—but find love
where they least expect it…

This month in

HER CELEBRITY SURGEON

Baron Rupert Charles Radley (aka Director of
Surgery) meets his match with fiery registrar
Dr Sophie Harrison. The paparazzi have a field-day!

And don't miss Sebastian's or Victoria's stories
coming in March and May 2006
only from Mills & Boon® Medical Romance™!

HER CELEBRITY SURGEON

BY
KATE HARDY

MILLS & BOON®

For Maggie, Sue and Sandy—with love

First published in Great Britain 2005
Paperback edition 2006
Harlequin Mills & Boon Limited,
Eton House, 18-24 Paradise Road, Richmond, Surrey TW9 1SR

© Pamela Brooks 2005

ISBN 0 263 84704 7

Set in Times Roman 10½ on 13 pt.
03-0106-50259

Printed and bound in Spain
by Litografia Rosés, S.A., Barcelona

CHAPTER ONE

HALF past eight. Sophie groaned inwardly. She'd probably missed the party for Guy's promotion to Director of Surgery, but no way could she have left her patient in the middle of the operating table. And she never, but never, left the ward until her patients had been round from the anaesthetic for at least half an hour. You never knew with surgery: one moment, your patient was fine; the next, all hell could be let loose and you might even need to go back into Theatre.

But when she finally made it into the wine bar opposite the hospital, Guy was on his own. 'Don't tell me that rotten lot went off to get food and gave you the short straw of waiting till I got here, when it's *your* party?' she asked.

'No. The party's off.'

'Why?'

He shrugged. 'The job went to an external candidate.'

'Oh, Guy. I'm so sorry.' He was a brilliant surgeon and a nice bloke, too. It really wasn't fair. 'I was so sure…'

'It means you're stuck where you are, too, Soph.'

Because she'd been in line for promotion to Guy's job. She waved her hand to protest at his bitter tone. 'Hey. My promotion wasn't a given, anyway. They couldn't advertise the job until your promotion had been announced—and I might not even have made it to the interview stage.' She could see in his face that he was brooding. And he'd had more than his share of hassles this year, with an acrimonious divorce. His wife had blamed her affair on Guy spending too much time on his career. Time that clearly hadn't paid off.

'Come on, let's have a commiseration drink instead. I'll shout you a curry. We can put the world to rights, and stick two fingers up at the hospital board—who clearly can't see talent when it's two millimetres in front of their noses.'

'You're good for my ego.'

Not as good as Abby would have been—Guy's house officer, who'd admitted to Sophie in the changing rooms a few weeks ago that she had the hots for Guy—but Sophie could work on that. A few judiciously dropped hints, and maybe Guy would see what was two millimetres in front of *his* nose.

When they'd settled themselves comfortably in the local curry house and ordered their meal, Sophie turned the conversation back to Guy's bad news.

'I hate to rub salt in your wounds, Guy, but do you know anything about the new director of surgery?'

'R. C. Radley, you mean?'

The name was familiar, but she couldn't think why. She nodded.

'He's a plastic surgeon.'

'We're going to have a nip-and-tuck merchant in charge of surgery? Oh, great. No prizes for guessing where all the new equipment's going to go, then.' Damn. And she'd raised half the money for the equipment she had her eye on. It looked as if she'd have to raise the other half, too.

'And he went to a certain well-known public school.'

Uh-oh. There was a distinct whiff of fish in the air. 'Eton?'

Guy nodded.

Like some of the members of the board. Sophie rolled her eyes. Now she understood what had been puzzling her—why Guy had been passed over. 'So the old-boy network strikes again, then?'

'Yep.'

'It sucks, Guy, it really does—but don't let it get to you. There'll be other chances.' She raised her glass of beer. 'Here's to us. You and me, and a brilliant surgical team.' Though she wasn't going to drink to their new director of surgery. Not until after she'd met him and seen if he was worth drinking to.

'Mr R. C. Radley. Why does his name ring a bell?' she asked.

'He's not a Mr. He's a lord.'

'He's a what?'

'A baron,' Guy told her.

Baron Radley? The board had appointed a *baron* to run the surgical team? Sophie's mouth tightened. 'So instead of giving the job to someone who can do it blindfolded, the board's made a political appointment. Someone who's got the right name and the right title.' And the right accent. Sharp, braying, coupled with a mocking, hearty guffaw as he... She shook herself. No. That had been years ago, and she was over it now. *Over* it.

'Soph, hang on. You're being a bit—'

'No, I'm absolutely right,' she cut in. 'They've gone for something that will bring some press coverage for the hospital, instead of thinking about what's right for the patients. And that stinks.' She frowned again. 'Baron Radley... Isn't he the one in all the gossip mags?' The ones her mum read. Now she remembered where she'd heard the name. *Celebrity Life.* Baron Radley had been photographed with just about every eligible woman in London—every woman with a title or who looked like a supermodel. There was a different woman on his arm every time he went somewhere. She shook her head in disbelief. 'Oh, for goodness' sake, what does the board think they're doing? We ought to—'

'Leave it, Soph,' Guy warned. 'Like you said, there'll be other chances. None of us can expect to get every job we go for.'

'But it's wrong. It's morally *wrong* that they've picked someone with a title instead of someone who can do the job.'

'He might be a good surgeon. And there's nothing we can do about it anyway.'

She sighed, knowing that he was right. 'At least, working in general surgery, we won't have to have much to do with him,' she said.

'Let's just forget about it, yeah?' Guy asked.

She nodded as their curry arrived, but the knot of tension at the back of her neck was starting to tighten again. How old was their new director of surgery exactly? Had he been one of the gang who…?

She wasn't going to think about them. It had been years ago. If she let the memories hold her back, they'd win. And she was damned sure they weren't going to grind her into the dust again. The chances were, R. C. Radley hadn't been one of them anyway. He was probably Guy's age, in his mid-to-late thirties—he'd probably finished med school before Sophie had even finished her A-levels. She certainly couldn't remember being at med school with anybody called Radley. And if he was older than she was, it was unlikely he'd been part of their social set either.

They kept the conversation on more neutral topics for the rest of the meal—avoiding hospital politics—but as they left the restaurant Sophie realised with dismay that Guy must have drunk several glasses of wine while he'd been waiting for her to turn up, as well as several beers during their meal.

Not only was he slightly unsteady on his feet but, when Sophie steadied his arm, he put his arms round her and tried to kiss her.

Sophie turned her face away so his lips landed wetly on her cheek. 'Come on, Guy. I'll call a cab to get you home.'

'Come home with me, Soph.'

'Not a good idea. You'd regret it in the morning.'

He smiled. 'Waking up to a gorgeous girl like you? No.'

She shook her head. 'Guy, it's the drink talking. I'm your mate, not your girlfriend. You used to be my boss, remember?'

'Not since you got promoted and moved over to Andy's team.'

Mmm, and she couldn't use the 'we can't mix work and a relationship' argument if she wanted to get him together with Abby—not when he was Abby's boss! 'I'm focusing on my career, Guy,' she said gently yet firmly.

'And because I didn't get the job, you're not interested?'

She narrowed her eyes. 'If I didn't think you're drunk and don't really know what you're saying, I'd slap your face for that. I don't sleep my way up the ladder, Guy. In fact, I don't do relationships at all, and you know that—my career comes first, last and always. We're friends, and I'd like to keep it that way.'

'Maybe I'd like more.'

The voices grated in her head again. *And I'm going to take it.*

She forced the memory back where it belonged. 'Not with me, you wouldn't. Guy, you're a nice bloke, but I'm not interested in anything more than friendship from you. From anyone.' She sighed. 'I'm beginning to think you're as short-sighted as the board.'

'Meaning?'

'Meaning that there are other women in our department. Women who might like you and be interested in having a relationship with you.'

'Like who?'

'I'm not telling you when you're drunk! Ask me when you're sober, and I might give you a clue.'

'Soph, you're a tease.'

And teases get what they ask for.

Again, she pushed the words away. 'Guy, just shut up and get in the taxi.' She bundled him into the back of the black cab she'd managed to hail, closed the door, gave Guy's address to the cabbie and paid him to take Guy home. Then she walked back to her own flat, made herself a strong cup of coffee and sifted through her post. Junk mail, more junk mail, a bank statement and a postcard from Sandy in Tokyo.

Sometimes she wished she'd had the nerve to do what her friend Sandy had done and taken a year out to travel. She could have rented her flat out for a year and gone round the world with Sandy. Had adventures. But, no, she'd been too staid and sensible. Surgical jobs weren't as easy to come by as emergency department jobs, so she'd declined Sandy's offer.

Did that make her boring? Maybe. But she'd worked hard to get as far as she had. Taking a year out would have set her back too much. She'd done the right thing.

Her mum had also popped round, found Sophie was out and had scribbled a note on the front cover of her favourite gossip magazine. *Missed you. Call me.* Sophie grinned. Typical. She'd even written her duty on her mother's kitchen calendar, so her mum would know know exactly when Sophie was likely to be at home—and Fran completely ignored it. Scatty didn't even begin to describe her. And Sophie adored her for it.

Idly, she sipped her coffee and flicked through the magazine. She really didn't understand what her mum saw in this kind of stuff. Who cared where celebs went or what their houses looked like?

Then a name leapt out at her.

Charlie, Baron Radley.

She stared at the photograph. He was dressed up to the nines—expensive dinner jacket, dress shirt, bow-tie. Tall, dark and handsome—and he looked as if he knew it, too. A woman in a little black dress—a dress she must have been poured into, and she was dripping in diamonds as well—was hanging off his arm. Her blonde hair was cut fashionably, her make-up was flawless and they really looked like the ultimate 'golden couple'.

The caption beneath, gushing about his fabulous wealth and his partner's equally fabulous modelling successes, didn't make Sophie feel any better about it. If anything, it convinced her even more that the board had made a terrible mistake. This man—one of the jet set, who went to all the best parties, probably only ever drank champagne and, for all she knew, might join the rest of his crowd in snorting the odd line of coke—was going to be the new director of surgery at the Hampstead General.

'This,' she predicted grimly, 'is going to end in tears.'

CHAPTER TWO

'SAMMY and I can't wait any longer,' Sophie said. 'We've got a patient prepped for Theatre and a huge list to get through.' It was all very well R.C. Baron Radley wanting to meet the team—but, if he couldn't even be bothered to turn up on time, why should their patients have to suffer?

'Sophie, don't you think you ought to give him another five minutes?' Abby said. 'I mean, Andy's off duty so you're the most senior one here from your firm. He's probably with one of the big cheeses—you know what they're like when they start talking. Give him five more minutes.'

Sophie shook her head. 'My patients come first. And if that gives me a black mark in Baron Radley's book, tough.' She curled her lip. 'I'm a doctor, not a serf who needs to bow down to the nobility.'

Guy whistled. 'Wow, Soph, I never knew you were so against titles.'

'I just don't see why an accident of birth makes one person "better"…' she emphasised the speech marks with two curled fingers on each hand '…than another. I'll just have to catch up with His Lordship later.'

'We'll give your apologies to him, Soph,' Abby said.

'I think,' Sophie said crisply, 'he should be the one apologising to us—and to our patients—for wasting time. See you later. Sammy, let's go scrub up.' Together with her house officer, she left the staffroom and headed for Theatre.

Something didn't look right, Charlie thought. The kid posting something through the neighbour's letterbox didn't have a bike with him or a bag full of newspapers. So just *what* was he stuffing through it?

Then there was a loud bang, and Charlie realised exactly what the boy had posted. A firework. It looked as if he had just taken another from his pocket. Hadn't anybody told him why it was stupid to play with fireworks? It was an explosive; it could go off in his face. And the one he'd shoved through the door could have done a lot of damage, too, if someone had been close to it when it had gone off. And you never, but never, lit fireworks with an ordinary match.

'Oi! What do you think you're doing?' he yelled.

The boy looked up, curled his lip, flicked a V-sign at Charlie and lit another match.

'Put that match out, you idiot! You'll get h—'

But before Charlie could finish, there was a loud bang and the firework in the boy's hand exploded.

Charlie forgot the fact that he was on his way to work—his first day in his new role as Director of Surgery, when he really shouldn't be late—and years of training took over. He grabbed his mobile phone and punched in the number for the emergency services as he ran towards the boy. 'Ambulance, please.' He gave them the location. 'We have a firework injury involving a child. Major burns.' Burns to the hand or feet were always classified as major. 'Better call the fire brigade, too—he was stuffing fireworks through a letterbox.'

The boy was screaming, and he'd dropped the match.

Luckily the ground was still wet, so the flame would have been extinguished—if any loose powder from the fireworks was lit, the boy could end up with flash burns to his legs as well as the damage to his hand.

Charlie pushed through the open gate just as the door to the neighbouring house opened.

'What's going on?' the elderly man demanded.

'Firework went off in his hand,' Charlie said swiftly. 'I've called the emergency services. I'm a doctor. Will you let me take a look?' he asked the boy.

Shaking, the boy held out his hands. 'It hurts!' he wailed.

'What's your name?' Charlie asked.

'L-Liam,' he choked.

'Bloody little hooligan! He's always causing trouble round here,' the neighbour said in disgust. 'We should just hand him over to the police.'

'Right now, my priority's to stop him losing blood. Have you got a first-aid kit?' Charlie asked.

'Only plasters and headache tablets.' The neighbour shrugged. 'The wife might have a bandage in there.'

Probably one that wasn't sterile, Charlie guessed. 'Do you have a clean, dry cloth—a teatowel or something? Please?'

The man nodded and went back inside his house. Meanwhile Charlie quickly assessed Liam's hand. Normally, in cases of thermal burns, you needed to cool the burn down fast with lukewarm water. But this wasn't a normal thermal burn—it had been caused by a firework. Fireworks often contained phosphorus, a chemical that reacted with water and caused more burning, so running water over the child's skin could do more damage.

From what he could see under the blood, the burn appeared to be full thickness, across the whole surface area of Liam's

hand, and two of his fingertips were missing. Gunpowder
residue was tattooed into the skin. They'd need to debride the
wound—cut away the damaged parts—and do a skin graft.
Probably more than one.

'OK, Liam. I know it's scary, but I'm going to look after
you until the ambulance gets here.' He needed to keep the boy
calm and stem the blood flow. 'Can you tell me your favourite football team?'

'M-Manchester United,' the boy stammered.

The knot at the back of Charlie's neck started to unravel.
Great. If he could get Liam talking, it would take the child's
mind off the injury. If Liam started panicking, there was more
chance he'd go into shock. Plus Charlie needed to know who
or what was behind that front door. The small pane of glass
in the centre of the door was opaque, so trying to look through
it wouldn't help. Had the firework set light to the carpet? Was
someone lying inside, hurt?

'Tell me about the players,' Charlie said.

The neighbour returned with a pile of dry teatowels. 'Will
these do? More than he deserves, mind. He's been persecut-
ing Mrs Ward for months.'

'She's an old cow. She—' Liam began, his face screwed
up in a mixture of scowling and pain.

'Later,' Charlie cut in. 'I need to clean any chemicals
from your hands, Liam. This might hurt, but I'll try to be
quick.' He looked at the neighbour. 'Do you know if Mrs
Ward is in?'

'Doesn't go out much. Dicky ticker.'

So the fright of a firework coming through her letterbox
could upset her enough to bring on her heart condition. 'Can you
try and get her to answer the door while I clean Liam's hand?'

The neighbour nodded. He banged on the door and called

through the letterbox, 'Mary, it's Bill—can you open the door?' Charlie quickly cleaned Liam's hand with one of the teatowels, then covered the wound with the other cloth. He pressed on it to stem the bleeding.

'No answer,' Bill said.

'OK.' It could be another ten minutes before the ambulance arrived. If Mary Ward had had a heart attack, Charlie needed to act now. 'I'll break in. Liam, can you press on that, hard?' he asked.

'It hurts,' Liam whimpered.

'I know, but we need to stop you losing blood. It's important—and I need to break this door down in case Mrs Ward's very ill.'

Liam hung his head. 'Is she going to die?'

'I hope not, for your sake. I'll tell the pol—' Bill began.

Charlie shook his head very slightly. They didn't have time to discuss that now. 'I really need to see if she's all right. Now, Liam, you keep pressing on that cloth. And keep telling me about Manchester United—it's really interesting.'

'Really?' Liam looked stunned, as if he wasn't used to anyone paying him proper attention.

Been there, done that, kid, Charlie thought. Though he'd never resorted to playing with fireworks to get the attention he'd needed. He'd just learned to become self-reliant.

'Keep talking,' he said, giving the boy an encouraging smile. If Liam kept talking, his voice would give Charlie warning signals if the boy was going into shock: the first signs would be if Liam started to sound 'spaced out' or his breathing became shallow.

'There are a couple of fingertips missing,' he said, *sotto voce,* to Bill. 'Could you try and find them for me and put them in a bag?' He could tell by the look on Bill's face that the elderly man thought it served the kid right. 'He's only a child,' Charlie said softly.

'He's a wrong 'un.'

'And he needs help. Please.'

Bill's mouth thinned, but he started to look through the weeds on the path.

Charlie crouched down to the letterbox. 'Mrs Ward? My name's Charlie and I'm a doctor. I'm coming to help you, but if you can't open the door for me I'll need to force it open.'

No reply. But at least he couldn't smell smoke either, so it seemed that the firework hadn't started a blaze. And he hadn't seen any orange flickers through the opaque glass or with the limited vision he'd had through the letterbox.

'I'm going to break the pane of glass and reach through to open the door,' Charlie said. 'Don't be frightened. Bill's with me.'

He took off one shoe, shattered the pane with it, then wrapped his hand in one of the teatowels to protect him from the broken glass and reached through to open the lock from the inside.

'Found them,' Bill said, at the precise moment Charlie pushed the door open to reveal a couple of burned-out bangers and scorch marks on the carpet.

'Let's go in and see to your neighbour.' Charlie shepherded Liam in before him. 'She'll probably have a plastic bag of some sort in her kitchen.' He hoped. And from the colour of the teatowel Liam was losing blood, which meant there was a good chance he'd go into shock. Charlie needed to get the boy lying flat, with his legs raised, as soon as possible: it would help to prevent shock from blood loss.

He found Mrs Ward slumped in the kitchen, her face white and her hand clutched to her chest.

'Mrs Ward, can you hear me?' he asked.

To his relief, Mrs Ward nodded.

'Mary! Oh, God, is she all right?' Bill asked.

'Bill, the best thing you can do to help is find a plastic bag and some ice for those fingertips. And can you get Liam to lie flat on his back with his legs raised? Try and keep pressure on that pad on his hand for me. I don't want him to lose consciousness.'

'But…' Bill gestured helplessly towards Mary.

'I'll look after her,' Charlie said quietly. 'I can't see to them both at the time same. I need you to help Liam. Please.'

Bill nodded and followed Charlie's directions. Meanwhile, Charlie checked Mary's pulse.

'Can you talk?' he asked Mary.

'Can't…breathe…' the old lady wheezed.

Breathless, pale and with obvious chest pain. Bill had mentioned his neighbour's 'dicky ticker'. Angina? 'Have you had pain like this before?' Charlie asked.

'Spray. Drawer,' the old lady whispered.

Which meant that, yes, she had and, yes, she had medication to deal with it. Good.

But there were several drawers to choose from. Which one? Charlie stood in the middle. 'Can you point me left or right, then put your hand up when I'm in front of the right drawer?' he asked.

She managed to direct him left and down to the drawer where she kept her medication. As he'd suspected, she had a GTN spray. Glyceryl trinitrate, known as GTN for short, increased the flow of blood through the heart muscle and controlled the symptoms of angina.

'Can you open your mouth and lift up your tongue for me, Mrs Ward?' he asked gently.

She did so, and he sprayed the medication under her

tongue—the quickest way to get the drug into her system. Hopefully the pain would ease very quickly. And where the hell was the ambulance?

'Little bugger. Right hooligan. Clip round the ear, if he was mine,' Mary muttered.

'Try not to talk,' Charlie soothed.

'Put fireworks through my door. Needs a good hiding,' she wheezed.

'He's learned his lesson the hard way,' Charlie said gently. 'One blew up in his hand. He's lost the tips of a couple of fingers.'

'Told him not to chuck rubbish in my garden. Kept on. Kicked my fence down. Now this.'

'The police'll sort it out, Mary,' Bill said. 'Oi, you, the doctor said to stay still!'

Charlie glanced over to see Liam struggling and Bill trying to pin him down.

'Can't stay. Mum'll kill me if I'm in trouble,' Liam said, clearly panicking.

'Should've thought of that earlier, shouldn't you?' Bill sneered. 'Tell that to them when they take you down the nick.'

'Liam, you'll be going to *hospital*,' Charlie interjected. 'We need to sort your hand out before anything else happens. And you need to stay calm right now. If you start moving about and lose much more blood, you'll start feeling very, very rough. Or you could struggle, and Bill will have to give you mouth to mouth.'

As he'd hoped, both Bill and Liam looked horrified at the thought. They both lapsed into silence, and Liam stayed absolutely still.

To Charlie's relief, he heard a shout at the front door. 'Paramedics—is anyone in there?'

'In the kitchen,' Charlie said.

'What have we got?' the older paramedic asked.

Charlie gave the two paramedics a brief run-down of what had happened. 'Mrs Ward's had GTN but it isn't having much effect. We've found Liam's missing fingertips and put them in a plastic bag with ice—I cleaned the wound with a dry cloth in case of phosphorus contamination.'

'Trained first-aider?' the younger paramedic asked.

Charlie smiled. 'Something like that.'

'We'll take them both in,' the older paramedic said.

'My house. Open,' Mary said.

'Don't worry, I'll stay and help the police secure it,' Bill said. 'I'll tell them what happened.'

Charlie took the notebook from his inside pocket and scribbled his mobile number. 'I need to get going, but they can get me on this number or call me at the hospital—the Hampstead General.'

'You work at our place?' the younger paramedic asked.

'Yep.' Charlie glanced at his watch. 'And I'd better get my skates on or I'll be late for work.' He was already late, but that couldn't be helped.

'Might as well come along with us, then,' the younger paramedic said with a smile.

Ten minutes after Sophie had left, Charlie walked into the department. 'Sorry I'm late. Unavoidable delay,' he said. Not that he was going to explain what his delay had been. *I had to rescue a woman with angina and a boy with major burns.* It would have sounded bleating or boastful or, worse, both together. 'Thanks for waiting. I wouldn't have blamed you all for getting on with your lists, thinking I wasn't going to bother turning up.'

Guy coughed. 'I'm afraid the other firm isn't here. Andy's away today and Sophie, his registrar, was called into Theatre.'

Pretty much as he would have expected. 'No problem. Hopefully I'll get a chance to catch up with them later.' Charlie shook his hand. 'Charlie Radley.'

'Guy Allsopp, consultant surgeon. This is Mark, my registrar, and Abby, my house officer,' Guy said. He quickly introduced the rest of the staff.

'Pleased to meet you all. Well, let's get the awkward stuff out of the way first,' Charlie said. 'First off, I know there were internal candidates for the job, so I imagine a few of you would much rather I wasn't here. I'm sorry that someone had to be disappointed, but I hope we can learn from each other and work as a team.'

He noticed that Guy and Abby exchanged very meaningful glances. Had Andy been an internal candidate and had he deliberately stayed away today? In that case, Sophie, as Andy's registrar, was showing solidarity with the head of her firm. They were the ones who really needed to hear this speech.

Ah, well. He'd make his peace with them both later. He had some other rumours to squash first.

'Secondly, I know what hospital rumour mills are like, so you're probably expecting a toff who spends more time with a string of blondes in little black dresses than with my patients, and who only does face lifts. I'm not planning to live up to those expectations. I'm here to do a job, I don't have a string of girlfriends, I answer to "Charlie", not "Your Lordship", and I don't do face lifts or nips and tucks.' He smiled. 'So. I hope we'll get used to each other pretty quickly. My door isn't always open because I think that's intimidating—but I'm always happy to talk through any problems between seeing patients.'

A few murmurs, but no outright hostility. Good. He could build on that.

'And, finally, so I can get to know people who aren't here today or are on a different shift, I'm planning drinks on Thursday night—my tab. If anyone can recommend a good bar, I'm all ears.' And, please, please, any minute now the emergency department would bleep him, he'd have to go to Theatre and he could just relax and do the job he loved.

'He's gorgeous,' Abby said.

'Guy? Yeah, you already told me. Several times,' Sophie said with a grin.

'No. I mean *Charlie*.'

'Charlie?'

Her puzzlement must have shown on her face, because Abby added, 'The new director of surgery.'

Ah. The baron. 'How nice for him,' Sophie said coolly.

Abby frowned. 'Don't be so hard on him. He's a nice bloke.'

He was upper class—and Sophie knew from experience just how *not* nice they could be. 'Yeah. I bet,' she said sarcastically, before she could stop herself.

'He is. He's buying drinks for everyone on Thursday night, and he's included the auxiliary staff and the cleaners,' Abby protested.

Sophie shrugged. 'So? He's a baron. Rich. He can afford it. It's an empty gesture, Abby.'

Abby frowned. 'He's not a snob, if that's what you're thinking. He's genuine.' She added what she clearly thought was her trump card: 'Guy likes him.'

'Well, that's all right, then, isn't it?' Sophie asked.

'Soph, I don't understand why you're so anti.'

'I'm not anti. I'm just saying I don't like politics and I don't think they have any place in hospitals. We should be looking after our patients, not playing games.'

'Charlie doesn't seem like a game-player.' Abby took a swig of her coffee. 'Let's agree to disagree, shall we?'

'I'll drink to that.' Sophie raised her own cup.

They'd been talking shop for about five minutes when a tray clattered onto the table next to theirs. 'Hi, Soph.'

'Hello, Guy.' She smiled at him. And then looked up at the man standing next to Guy—into the bluest eyes she'd ever seen.

Baron R. C. Radley.

The photographs in the gossip rags simply didn't do him justice. In the press he always looked slightly unreal—with a perfect tan, even white teeth and not so much as a faint shadow under his eyes or a blemish on his skin.

In the flesh, he was something else. Tall—about six feet two, she'd guess—with dark hair cut just a little bit too short. Sculpted cheekbones, a haughty nose—very patrician. Except his lower lip was full and gave him a slightly vulnerable air, and there were tiny lines at the corners of his eyes that told her that he smiled a lot.

Her pulse started to hammer, and the back of her neck tingled. Gorgeous didn't even begin to describe him. Neither did mouth-watering. He was both—and more.

Please, don't let her mouth be hanging open.

'Let me introduce you,' Guy said. 'Soph, this is Charlie. Charlie, this is Sophie Harrison, the senior registrar on Andy's team.'

Charlie placed his tray carefully on the table and held his hand out. 'Pleased to meet you. And I'm sorry I missed you this morning.'

He had a posh voice. The sort that usually raised her hackles. So why did she suddenly want to purr? Not good. Not good at all.

Sophie was aware that Abby and Guy were both staring at her. Oh, yes. She was meant to shake the baron's hand. Though when she did, she wished she hadn't. Her skin was actually *tingling* where it had touched him.

No way. She wasn't going to fall under the spell of someone like him—a womaniser *and* a toff. Absolutely not. 'Sorry I couldn't wait.' For you to bother to turn up. 'I had a full list.'

'Of course. Patients are nervous enough before an operation—the last thing they need are unexpected delays.'

Not quite the reaction she'd been expecting. Wasn't he supposed to be offended that she hadn't waited to tug her forelock?

Before she could reply, one of the nurses came over. 'Hey, Charlie!'

Batted eyelashes—and Sophie would bet that the nurse had just breathed in hard. Certainly, her bust was difficult to ignore. Her name tag said that she was from the emergency department. Don't say their new director of surgery had already started working his way through the nurses?

'I thought you might like to know how Mrs Ward's getting on. She's stable and we're sending her home.'

'That's good,' Charlie said.

'How's Liam?' she asked.

'Out of Theatre. Guy did a good job.'

Sophie frowned. 'Am I missing something here?'

'Didn't he tell you?' the nurse asked. 'Our Charlie's a hero. He was on his way in this morning when he saw this kid stuffing fireworks in this old lady's letterbox. One went off in the boy's hand—and the old lady had angina. Charlie rescued them both.'

'You didn't tell me you were involved in the rescue as well,' Guy said. 'So that's why you were late this morning?'

Charlie shrugged. 'I just called the ambulance, as anyone else would have done.'

'Don't be modest.' The nurse batted his protest away. 'The paramedics reckon you're a hero. The papers have been ringing up, too—they want a picture of you.'

So this was what it was all about. Baron Radley, Hero of Hampstead. A PR opportunity. The hospital would be delighted to get some positive press instead of pointed comments about superbugs, declining standards and lengthening waiting lists.

'They're not getting a picture. And the press office can handle the calls,' Charlie said. 'I'm a doctor. I did what any other doctor would have done. That's all.'

All? Sophie didn't think so. He might be a doctor—but he was one with a title. And one who'd been linked in the press with too many gorgeous women to count.

He flashed a smile—one she'd bet he'd practised. A lot. 'But thanks for telling me about Mrs Ward.'

It was a dismissal, and the nurse knew it. 'See you later, Charlie.' She actually gave him a coy little wave. What was it about this man that fried women's brain cells? Sophie wondered in disgust.

Though that smile was definitely a lethal weapon. She'd have to be careful. Very careful.

'So what happened?' Abby asked.

'Full-thickness burns to the palm of the dominant hand and two amputated fingertips. Guy did an excellent job of debridement and repairing the fingertips,' Charlie said.

'And Charlie did the skin grafts.'

Usually, skin grafts were delayed for a couple of weeks after the burn, when the dead skin started sloughing off—but in certain cases, such as fingers and eyelids, primary skin grafts had to be made as soon as possible after the injury to reduce the likelihood of infection.

'I assume he's staying in Paeds for a few days?' Sophie asked. Burns to the hand were very difficult to manage at home, and there was a high risk of infection by *Streptococcus pyogenes* in the first week. The boy would definitely be on a course of antibiotics to reduce the risk of infection.

Charlie nodded. 'I want to keep a check on him in case of fibrotic contractions.' The fibres around the burn often contracted as they healed, and could cause problems with movement. The likelihood was that the boy would need multiple plastic surgery operations. 'Plus he needs to keep his hand elevated.' That would reduce the risk of swelling, or oedema, which could cause problems as the burn healed.

'I think you've made a hit in ED,' Guy said.

Charlie grinned. 'They'll get over it. When people get to know me better, they'll realise I'm just like any other surgeon around here.'

Like any other? Hmm. Sophie didn't think so.

'I'm happiest when I've got a scalpel in my hand,' Charlie added. 'Now, please, let the coffee here be better than at my last place…'

Smooth. Very, very smooth.

But Sophie wasn't tugging her forelock to anyone.

She gave him a cool little smile, and turned her attention back to her lunch.

CHAPTER THREE

'I CAN'T believe Tom didn't even notice his foot was gangrenous!' Abby said.

'Type-one diabetic, male, early thirties, single, lives on his own—no, I can buy it,' Sophie said.

Abby shook her head. 'I can't, even though I know people with diabetes are more at risk of foot infections and ulcers—their circulation doesn't work properly and it affects the motor, sensory and autonomic nerves.'

'Which means?' Sophie asked.

'The motor nerves supplying the small muscles of the foot and the calf don't work properly so the weight-bearing bit of the foot is distorted,' Abby recited. 'The effect on the autonomic nerves means the foot doesn't sweat, and the sensory nerves don't work so the patient doesn't feel any pain.'

'Exactly.' Sophie thought Abby was shaping up to be an excellent doctor—she knew the textbook stuff. Now she just needed to understand her patients a bit more and empathise with them. 'You don't feel it, so you don't do anything about it. Nearly half the time diabetic patients spend in hospital is because of foot problems.'

'But surely he must have *seen* it?' Abby asked.

'He probably hoped it would just go away on its own. A

lot of people do—they're scared of doctors and hope if they ignore the problem it'll go away.'

Abby shook her head in disgust. 'So why didn't his diabetic nurse pick it up?'

'Because,' Sophie said, 'he didn't turn up for any of his appointments. He got divorced last year and his mum told me yesterday he cut himself off from the rest of the world. The only reason we know about his foot is because he had a hypoglycaemic attack at work and the foreman insisted on him coming to hospital. Lucky ED was clued up enough to guess if he wasn't keeping his glucose levels under proper control, he probably wasn't looking after himself and might have a bit of ulceration on his feet as well.'

'*A bit of ulceration?* Soph, the entire dorsum of his foot is necrotic!' Abby said, aghast.

'Yup.' The top of Tom's foot was red, swollen and puffy, and the tissue beneath was dead. 'The sad thing is, it could all have been avoided if he'd come for treatment earlier.' Sophie sighed. 'The gangrene's too bad for me to save his foot. I just wish I could have done reconstructive surgery on it—which I would have been able to do if he'd seen us weeks ago. He might have lost a toe or two, but it would still have been workable. Whereas this… It's going to take him months of physiotherapy to get used to a false leg.'

'What does Charlie say?'

'Same as me. It has to come off.' Sophie had checked with him the previous afternoon, and together they'd explained the options to Tom. She'd been impressed by the way Charlie had handled it and had tried to give Tom some dignity. 'He's doing the op with me this afternoon. We've been giving Tom an epidural for the last twenty-four hours.'

'Why?'

'Studies show he's less likely to suffer from phantom limb pain after the amputation,' Sophie explained. 'We're going to do a below-knee amputation—I need to go high enough to make sure the tissue I cut through is healthy. Why?'

'Because otherwise there's a risk the wound will break down and become ulcerated, so you have to do another amputation. You're going below the knee—mid-tibia—because it'll improve his mobility with a prosthesis,' Abby added.

'Perfect textbook answer,' a voice said beside them.

Sophie did her best to ignore the tingling at the back of her neck. Charlie was just another one of the team, and she was going to treat him accordingly. He was just another doctor. So what if he had the sexiest mouth she'd ever seen? So what if his neck just invited you to caress it? The two of them were worlds apart, and it would stay that way.

'Want to come and watch, if Guy can spare you?' Charlie asked. 'The full op takes about an hour and a half, but if he can only spare you for part of it, that's fine.'

'Could I?' Abby beamed at him. 'I'll go and ask Guy!'

When she'd gone, that left Charlie and Sophie together. Alone.

Well, they had to work together. Just because she didn't like what he stood for, it didn't mean she'd be deliberately obstructive—not where work was concerned. Patients took priority in Sophie's eyes.

'How's Tom?' Charlie asked.

'Pretty miserable. And wishing he'd seen a doctor earlier,' Sophie said wryly.

'Poor bloke. But there was too much necrosis for us to be able to save the foot.' He looked at Sophie. 'You didn't mind me asking Abby if she wanted to watch, did you?'

'No. It's good experience for her.' And he had at least said it was on condition Guy could spare his house officer. He wasn't just expecting everyone to drop everything because the director of surgery said so.

'I noticed you coaching her just then,' Charlie added.

Sophie shrugged. 'Just doing my job.'

'Some surgeons hate dealing with junior doctors.'

'Abby's keen, bright and fits in well with the team. I'm more than happy to help,' she said stiffly.

There had definitely been an undercurrent to her words. What? Was she saying she didn't think *he* fitted in with the team? Charlie sighed inwardly. He hadn't been there long enough to know if he'd fit in or not. But Sophie wasn't even giving him a chance. He'd been drawn to her when he'd overheard her coaching Abby—the encouragement in her voice, the smile on her face, those beautiful brown eyes lively as she'd talked about the operation. He hadn't been able to stop himself joining in.

And she'd frozen on him completely.

Until that moment he'd had no idea how cold brown eyes could be.

But he'd never met her before yesterday. He was sure of that: Sophie Harrison was definitely a woman he'd remember. So it couldn't be anything he'd done personally to upset her.

It had to be the baron thing.

OK. He'd deal with it. After the operation he'd pull rank, take her for a coffee and straighten things out between them.

For professional reasons, of course. He wasn't stupid enough to get involved with somebody he worked with. Unlike his younger brother, he didn't mix work and play. Even though Sophie Harrison pressed all his buttons. Long blonde hair she kept caught back from her face with a clip in a way that made him want to remove it and run his fingers through it. Deep brown eyes he could drown in. And a perfect Cupid's-bow mouth that made him want to cup her face in his hands and kiss her.

And if he did it, he had the feeling she'd break both his legs.

Professionally, they might be able to work together. Social-ly, no chance. So he wasn't even going to go there.

'I'll see you in Theatre, then,' he said.

'Sure.'

Was it his imagination, or was there relief on her face—relief that he hadn't suggested having lunch together? Sup-pressing the sting of hurt, he walked away. It wasn't personal. He needed to find some middle ground, some way for them to work together. It'd take time. He just had to accept that and live with her suppressed hostility in the meantime.

Sophie's spine tingled as she walked into the changing rooms. It was the adrenalin rush she always had before an operation, the one that kept her on the top of her game. When she'd worked with Guy, he'd always said that the day she stopped being nervous before an operation was the day she should hang up her scrubs—because you should never, ever take anything for granted in surgery. Even apparently routine jobs could suddenly change, develop an unexpected complication.

She changed quickly, tucked her hair into a cap, put her mask on and went to scrub up. Charlie was already there—clearly he'd already done his nails and the initial wash because he was scrub-bing his hands and forearms. Nice forearms, she thought absent-ly. Strong. Nice hands, too, strong and capable. For one shocking moment she actually wondered what they'd feel like on her skin.

Then she shook herself. It wasn't going to happen. She'd sworn that his type would never touch her again.

Once they'd finished scrubbing up and were gowned, gloved and masked, they went into the operating theatre. Tom had had the choice of a spinal block or general anaesthetic— he'd opted for a general. It carried more risks than a spinal, but she could understand that he didn't want to know what was going on. How could you just lie there as a surgeon removed your foot and half your lower leg? Even though you wouldn't be able to feel it and the anaesthetic meant you wouldn't be able to move anyway, you'd know exactly what was happening. You'd hear *everything*.

And it would be unbearable.

'Poor man. He's got a tough time ahead of him,' she said.

'What's going to happen after the operation?' Abby asked.

'We'll check his bandages aren't too tight after about eight hours, then remove the drains a bit later without disturbing the dressings. In a couple of days he'll start gentle physiotherapy to make sure there are no contractures at the hip or knee joints. And we need to get in touch with the limb-fitting and rehab departments as soon as possible,' Sophie explained.

'Over to you, Dr Harrison,' Charlie said quietly.

Sophie checked that the anaesthetists were happy to proceed. 'OK, Abby, I'll talk you through what we're going to do. In the old days they used to just slice off the limb and leave it to heal—it reduced the risk of gas gangrene or tetanus, but it was hopeless trying to fit a prosthesis to the limb.'

Charlie would be the best one to explain about the skin flap. But what did she call him? Mr Radley? She wasn't up on Debrett's, so she didn't know what you were supposed to call a baron, but she was pretty sure it wouldn't be 'Mr'. Did she copy his formality or strike a blow for the common people and call him 'Charlie'?

In the end, she went for a cop-out. 'Our director of surgery will explain about the skin flaps.'

Then she made the mistake of glancing up. All she could see were his eyes above his surgical mask. Gorgeous slate-blue eyes. *Sexy* slate-blue eyes. But there was also a glint of amusement there. Was he laughing at her?

Just like his type had laughed at her before. She lifted her chin. 'Problem, Radley?'

'No, Harrison.'

He was definitely laughing at her, and Sophie scowled as she made the first incision.

'Abby, the blood supply to the tissues of the lower leg is better at the front than at the back, so what I'm going to do is something called a "skew flap". It's a long posterior flap of muscle, with equal skin flaps. Harrison's going to cut about twelve centimetres below the tibial tuberosity, so it preserves the patient's knee joint and makes rehabilitation easier.'

He was following her lead and referring to her by her surname. Fine. She could cope with that. It felt rude—insulting, almost—but, then again, she'd started it.

'We'll have the drains out in the first couple of days and the sutures out in ten days to two weeks,' Sophie added. 'But he'll be on the ward for two or three weeks.'

Then it was the bit she hated: cutting the bone. Even after all her years of experience she still hated the sound of bone being sawn through. But she concentrated on what she was doing, talking Abby through it.

When Charlie took over to deal with the skin flap, she noticed how deft and capable his hands were. Whatever her issues were with him as a person, she respected the way he worked. And she liked the way he treated the scrub nurses—

with courtesy, rather than shouting at them or giving curt, dismissive orders.

Maybe, just maybe, she'd got him wrong. Maybe he wasn't like all the other toffs she'd met at med school.

Or maybe he was. Maybe this was just a smokescreen. All charm, to hide what he was really like underneath. How could she trust him? How could she trust *anyone* from his class?

Guy had given Abby the time to watch the whole operation. To Sophie's surprise, Charlie let the young house officer do some of the suturing. 'Guy says your knots are good. Let's see how you do with this one.'

Abby was clearly delighted at the chance. Although she worked slowly, her knots were good, and as her confidence grew with Charlie's praise, the speed of her suturing increased.

'Well done,' Charlie said. 'I think she did well—don't you, Harrison?'

'I do, Radley.'

Just as she'd finished changing, Charlie walked over to her. 'Come and have a coffee while we're waiting for Tom to wake up.'

'I've got paperwork to do.'

'Paperwork can wait.'

'I really don't need a coffee.'

'You've just spent an hour and a half in Theatre. You need a break. Ten minutes. That's all I'm asking.'

He was asking? It sounded more like a demand to her.

'I think,' he said quietly, 'we need to talk. My office or the canteen. Your choice. But I could do with a coffee.'

There was nothing to say. Why did he think they needed to talk?

'Canteen, then,' she muttered, knowing that she sounded childish. But Charlie Radley rubbed her up the wrong way.

* * *

She really didn't want to be there with him. That much was obvious. And he could tell that she was going to insist on buying her own coffee. Well, he wasn't in the mood for politics of any sort. When they got to the cash till, he glared at her—and the glare worked. She shut up and let him pay.

They walked in silence to a quiet corner table.

'Right. Cards-on-table time,' he said. 'I know everyone expected Guy to get the director of surgery post. I know you were in line to get Guy's job. I'm sorry that your plans didn't work out, but that's the way of the world. Sometimes new blood can be good for a department.'

She snorted. 'Right.'

'And your point is?'

'You're a nip-and-tuck man. It's obvious where the money's going to go.'

'I'm a plastic surgeon, yes. But I don't do nips or tucks. I don't do cosmetic surgery, except in cases of trauma or where there's a medical reason for it. And the budget for this year was set before I arrived.'

She took a deep breath. 'Next year's money, then.'

'Next year's budget,' Charlie said calmly, 'will be allocated in terms of need. And I'll be discussing it with Guy and Andy before I make final decisions. Clear?'

'Clear.'

'Good. So what's the rest of your problem?'

'What do you mean?'

Nicely parried. She hadn't denied there was a problem, but she'd shifted the onus on him to say what he thought. OK. He'd play it straight. 'You don't like me, Sophie Harrison. Now, I know we've never met before, so I can't have upset you personally. What's the problem?'

She lifted her chin, and there was a definite spark of challenge in her eyes. 'OK. You want to know? I think the board appointed you for political reasons.'

He rolled his eyes. 'Oh, you mean the "lord" bit. Well, if you'd been there when I arrived yesterday, you'd have heard me tell everyone I don't use it. I answer to Charlie.'

'If you'd been on time yesterday,' she pointed out, 'I wouldn't have been in Theatre.'

'Unfortunately, I was delayed.'

'Your hero rescue work.'

Oh, please. She didn't think he'd set it up…did she? 'What would you have done?' he asked. 'It's your first day in a new job—a job where you know most of the staff don't want you there. A child is stuffing fireworks through a letterbox, but one blows up in his hand. If you stop to help, you're going to be late and your new team's going to think you're too arrogant to care, which means your first day is going to be even worse than you expect. So do you just leave the kid—and whoever's inside the house, who might also be hurt—or do you call an ambulance and do what you can on the first-aid front? Especially knowing that the general public would pour water or milk on a burn because that's what all the first-aid stuff says they should do?'

'Which would be the worst thing they could do to a burn contaminated with phosphorus.' She sighed. 'OK. I'd have done what you did.'

'Thank you.' Charlie leaned back in his chair. 'I don't want to fight with you, Sophie—may I call you Sophie?'

She nodded.

'As for the "lord" bit—it's simply an accident of birth.'

Uh-oh. The words were identical to the ones she'd used yesterday morning. Had someone repeated her comment to him?

And why did it make her feel suddenly guilty? She stuck by what she'd said. Why should you be treated differently because you came from a posh background?

'Don't hold my background against me,' Charlie said quietly, almost as if he'd read her mind. 'It's not a privilege, it's a handicap. People think I've been promoted because of who I am, not what I can do. I worked hard to get my degree, and I worked hard to get my position. And then I have to work a little bit harder still to prove it to everyone else.'

Pretty much as female surgeons had to—there was still a glass ceiling. To get to the very top as a surgeon, you had to forget about career breaks and children and family. You had to be twice as dedicated as any man.

Prejudice cut two ways. Sophie flushed. And she'd definitely been prejudiced against Charlie. She hadn't given him a proper chance.

'I'm a doctor. It's what I wanted to be—who I am.'

And he meant it. His voice was absolutely sincere.

'I…I'm sorry.'

'Apology accepted. Hopefully things will be straight between us now.'

He didn't sound as if he was gloating. He sounded…relieved.

'I like the way you work,' he added. 'No fuss, no drama, no lording it over junior staff.'

At the word 'lord', she met his gaze again. His eyes crinkled at the corners—he was laughing again. But at himself, not at her.

Almost unwillingly, she found herself smiling back. 'I'm the wrong sex to lord it. Lady it, perhaps?'

The smile in his eyes spread to his mouth, and she wished she hadn't made him grin like that. Because it made him appeal to her more than any man she'd ever met.

It wasn't going to happen. Charlie Radley had been photographed with more women than she'd had hot dinners. Women of his kind—the supermodels and debutantes. Sophie knew she wasn't in the same league; besides, she didn't want a quick affair. She didn't want any kind of affair. She just wanted to do her job, and do it well.

'Given the chance,' Charlie said, 'I think I'm going to like you. Working with you, I mean,' he added.

Given the chance. The rest of the team seemed to like him. And she'd been impressed by the way he worked in Theatre. Cool, calm, very sure of his skill, but equally concerned that his team should know everything that was going on. Including the nurses. 'So let's take each other at face value,' she suggested.

He nodded, and lifted his coffee-cup. 'Here's to a working relationship. Straightforward and honest. Mutual respect for each other's expertise and judgement.'

She could drink to that. She lifted her own coffee-cup. 'Cheers.'

'And maybe,' Charlie said softly, 'in the end you won't dislike me so much after all.'

CHAPTER FOUR

OVER the next few days, Charlie settled in with the rest of the team. Sophie even worked with him a couple of times without her hackles rising, although she still avoided Charlie's drinks night on the Thursday. Being off duty was a good enough excuse, as far as she was concerned. Although he gave her a quizzical look when they were next on the ward together, at least he didn't take her to task for it.

Then she got a call from Paul, the registrar in the emergency department. 'Twelve years old, fell from a horse which then stood on her. Admitted with bruising over her lower ribs and tachychardia. I think she's ruptured her spleen. Any chance of doing a laparotomy?'

'I'll organize Theatre,' Sophie said. 'Have you done a CT scan?'

'Too long a wait. I did a peritoneal lavage,' Paul said. 'We had blood staining.'

Blood staining indicated an internal injury to the abdomen, and bruising over the lower ribs was often associated with damage to the spleen, liver or kidney.

'One other thing,' Paul added, lowering his voice. 'The mum's a Jehovah's Witness. So is the girl.'

'Ah.' That was a possible sticking point. If the girl needed to have her spleen removed, she might need a blood transfusion—which was unacceptable on religious grounds to most Jehovah's Witnesses, who interpreted blood transfusion as the 'eating of blood'. Autologous transfusion, where the patient's own blood was salvaged during an operation and filtered, ready for reuse, was a possible solution, but some patients would find that unacceptable if the blood had left the blood vessels rather than being in continual contact with the patient's own circulation.

There were alternatives, such as the use of recombinant human erythropoietin, a hormone that helped red blood cells to reproduce. This helped to avoid anaemia around the time of the operation. But it really depended on what happened during the operation.

Sophie bit her lip. She hated cases like this. Ethically, she was bound to defer to the patient's wishes, but it was a grey area in the case of children. Children under the age of sixteen could consent to blood transfusions but couldn't refuse one. But if the parents were staunch believers, the surgeon had to either abide by their wishes or apply to the courts. In an emergency Sophie knew she could give a child blood without legal consent—if she let the child bleed to death, apart from being against her personal ethics, it could leave her open to legal prosecution for negligence. But if she did give the transfusion, that would leave an emotional minefield.

It *would* have to happen on Andy's day off. Guy was in Theatre. Maybe she could buzz through and get a lead from him. 'I'm on my way,' she said grimly, and replaced the receiver.

She pushed through the doors to leave the department, and almost walked straight into Charlie.

'You OK?' he asked.

She nodded. 'ED called. There's a twelve-year-old girl with a possible ruptured spleen and they want me to take a look.'

'Complications?'

How had he guessed? Or did he respect her skill enough to think she could do a splenectomy without problems? 'Mum's religious beliefs. If I have to do a splenectomy, it'll have to be without a transfusion.'

'Ah. Just the mum, or the dad as well?'

'I don't know right now,' she said honestly. 'I'm guessing it's both of them.' If the girl's father was of a different religion—one that didn't have the same issues with blood transfusion—she might be able to get his consent. Which would be enough. She only needed the consent of one parent.

'Want some back-up?'

She was tempted to say no, she could cope on her own; her pride said she shouldn't accept help from him. Her common sense gave her pride a swift upper-cut. She would have asked Andy or Guy for help. Charlie was here, and he was senior to both Andy and Guy. So what was the difference? 'Yes. Please,' she added.

'What are your plans?' he asked as they headed towards ED.

'I'm going to examine the girl and explain the situation to her parents—that I'll do my best to do the operation without any transfusions, respecting their wishes, but if there's a complication a transfusion might be unavoidable.' She sighed. 'It's not my place to judge, but I just don't understand how a parent could stand by and watch her child bleed to death.'

'Most parents find it acceptable if you say you'll do your best not to use a transfusion, but you won't allow the child to die for want of a transfusion,' Charlie said softly. 'Besides, all treatment is confidential.'

'I just hope they see it that way,' Sophie said feelingly. 'I'd move mountains for my child.'

For *her* child? Charlie's heart missed a beat. Sophie was married? But he'd been so sure she wasn't. He hadn't heard anyone talk about her partner or children. He glanced surreptitiously at her left hand. A surgeon never wore rings to work, but maybe Sophie wore a wedding ring on a chain around her neck or something. He couldn't see any band of pale skin on her ring finger, so maybe she was divorced. Single mum?

'Boy or girl?' he asked, trying to sound relatively cool.

'Pardon?'

'You said you'd move mountains for your child. I just wondered if you had a boy or a girl.' Now he was beginning to wish he'd never asked. She'd think he was being nosy. And just why was he asking anyway? It was none of his business.

She shrugged. 'I don't have any children. I was speaking figuratively. My parents moved mountains for me—we couldn't really afford for me to go to med school, despite the student grants and hardship funds, but they both took on extra jobs in the evenings to raise the cash. Mum cleaned and Dad did a few shifts behind the bar at the local pub, and I did bar work in the holidays and at weekends.'

Ouch. No wonder she'd been a bit hostile towards him. A lot of the medical students he remembered had come from rich backgrounds. But he couldn't think of many whose parents would have made the extra sacrifices that Sophie's parents had made. His mother certainly wouldn't have. He, Seb and Vicky had had to fight all the way, too, to get to med school.

Not that he was going to share *that* with Sophie. He didn't think she'd believe him somehow.

Her parents' lack of wealth also explained why Sophie Harrison was so ambitious, so focused on her job. Clearly she wanted to show her parents that their sacrifices had been worth it. Again, he wasn't going to tell her he'd worked that out. It would sound too patronising, even though he wouldn't mean it that way. 'I'd imagine they're very proud of you,' he said lightly.

'I'm proud of them,' Sophie responded crisply.

Family meant a lot to her. And he envied her for it. He was close to Seb and Vicky, though even that was a complicated mixture of sibling rivalry and watching each other's backs. But his mother… They hadn't been close for years and years. Since his father's death. Maybe even before that, if he thought about it.

Not that he was going to. He preferred to keep that shut well away. Where it was safe.

'Are you an only child?' he asked.

'Why?'

'Just making conversation.' Trying to find out more about her. Stupid, really. They'd never be anything more than colleagues. Probably not even friends. He'd noticed that she'd avoided his drinks night, when other colleagues who'd been off duty had turned up.

'Yes. I think my parents wanted more, but they just weren't lucky. You?'

She actually wanted to know something about him? He suppressed a flare of pleasure. She was probably just being polite. Making conversation. 'I'm the oldest of three. My brother's in emergency medicine, and our baby sister's the clever one. She's a brain surgeon.'

She looked at him, then, though he couldn't tell her thoughts from her expression. 'A brain surgeon.'

'Yep. We tease her a bit—you know, "our sister, the brain surgeon"—but Seb and I are really proud of her. Vicky's a brilliant neurologist.'

'The gossip rags never talk about them.'

Then she looked horrified, as if she'd given too much away.

Charlie's heartbeat quickened. Had she read them, looking for him?

No, of course not. Don't be so arrogant, he told himself sharply. Sophie was much too serious to read gossip rags. Anyway, she'd been talking about his siblings. 'They don't. Probably because Vicky would break the fingers of any paparazzi who dared to take a picture of her, and Seb's got the mouth of a lawyer.' He sighed. 'And they're not the ones stuck with—' He clammed up. Sophie definitely wouldn't be interested in what it was really like to be a baron. How everyone wanted to be your friend, just so they could say they were friends with the nobility. How the estate was an albatross around his neck—a place he hardly ever went nowadays, although he'd loved it as a child. It hadn't been his home for well over a decade, but he wasn't about to throw his mother out or expect her to deal with the upkeep. It was his responsibility. And also the reason why, on a consultant surgeon's salary, he had less money to spare than a house officer.

'Stuck with what?' she asked.

'Nothing,' he muttered. 'Just stuff. And we've got a patient to see.'

Well, *her* patient.

In the ED, Paul introduced them to Katrina, who was white with pain.

'Katrina, may I examine you?' Sophie asked.

The girl nodded. Sophie examined her as gently as she

could, noting that the girl's ribs were discoloured, there was localised tenderness and guarding in her abdomen and pain in the upper left quadrant.

'Does it hurt anywhere else?' Sophie asked.

'My shoulder. The left one.'

Kehr's sign, meaning that there was definitely a problem with Sophie's spleen. In addition to that, Katrina's abdomen was distended and Sophie already knew there was an internal bleed, thanks to Paul's lavage.

'Mr and Mrs Jackson, I think your daughter has a ruptured spleen,' Sophie explained to Katrina's parents. 'She's going to need an operation.'

'She can't have a transfusion,' Mrs Jackson said immediately. 'We're Jehovah's Witnesses. It's against our religion.'

'I'll do my best to respect your wishes,' Sophie said. 'I need to take a closer look—I'll do a procedure called a laparotomy. It's a small incision in her stomach, and it will show me how bad the damage is. I may be able to glue it back together if the damage isn't too bad, but I might need to remove her spleen.'

'She can't have a transfusion,' Mrs Jackson repeated.

'As I said, I'll respect your wishes as far as I can,' Sophie replied.

'If there are complications during surgery and she needs blood, she could die without a transfusion,' Charlie warned quietly.

Mrs Jackson's face was set. 'I know my rights. You can't give her a transfusion without my permission, and I won't give it.'

'I know. But I have responsibilities to my patient, too. In an emergency, my priority will be to save your daughter's life,' Sophie explained.

'If it's willed…' Mrs Jackson shook her head. 'No.'

'All right, Mrs Jackson. If you'll excuse me, I just need a word with my consultant.' Sophie looked at Charlie and slid her eyes sideways, indicating that she wanted a word away from the Jacksons.

'What?' he asked softly.

'I've got a hunch that Katrina's dad doesn't feel the same way as his wife. Can you do me a favour and keep Mrs Jackson talking while I have a quick word with Mr Jackson?'

'Sophie, you're opening a can of worms here,' Charlie warned.

'What's the choice? A row between the parents or the unnecessary death of a child. I know where my vote goes. We haven't got time to fight. Please. Just keep her talking.'

He nodded. 'I'll explain autologous transfusion and see what her views are on that. But if you get the slightest indication from Katrina's father that you're going the wrong way, stop. We'll get a co-ordinator in to do the talking for us.'

'But—'

'No arguments, Sophie.'

His accent was suddenly cut-glass, and it raised her hackles—particularly as she knew he was right. 'OK. I'll tread carefully,' she promised.

While Charlie talked to Mrs Jackson, Sophie drew Katrina's father to one side. 'Mr Jackson, you know that the treatment we give people is confidential, don't you? The only people who will know anything about Sophie's treatment are you and your wife.'

He nodded. 'My wife's a Jehovah's Witness.'

Meaning that he wasn't? 'Do you share your wife's beliefs?' Sophie asked carefully.

He closed his eyes. 'No. She was converted by some

friends. She was depressed after Katrina was born, but going to meetings made her happy again, so I went along with it.' He opened his eyes again and looked at Sophie. 'Could Katrina die if she doesn't have a transfusion?'

She had to be honest with him. 'I won't know until she's in Theatre. But it's a possibility, yes. If she needs a transfusion and I can't give it to her…' She spread her hands. 'That's the worst-case scenario. Hopefully it won't come to that.'

He shuddered. 'I don't want her to die.'

'This isn't about a battle of wills or judging your wife. But I want to give Katrina the best treatment available. We only need one parent to agree,' Sophie said softly. 'I know it could make things difficult between you and your wife.'

'Katrina comes first. I'll sign the consent form,' he said.

'Thank you,' she said quietly. 'I won't say anything to your wife. It might not even come to this. But if it does—it's good to know there's a safety net there.'

But Mrs Jackson had clearly anticipated Sophie's move. 'If you sign that form, Derek, I'll make sure you never see Katrina again.'

Mr Jackson paled. 'Alice, be reasonable. Katrina's life could be at stake.'

'If it's a bad rupture, she could bleed to death,' Sophie said quietly. 'And I need to take her to Theatre now.'

Charlie stepped in. 'Maybe we can do the autologous transfusion we talked about.'

Alice Jackson's face set. 'Maybe.'

'Mrs Jackson, I will do my best to abide by your wishes,' Sophie said, 'but as a surgeon I cannot allow your daughter to die due to the lack of a transfusion.'

'BP's dropping,' Charlie said quietly. 'Mrs Jackson, we have to go to Theatre now.'

'You're doing the operation? I've seen you in the papers. Out with all those women.' She shook her head. 'No. I don't want you touching my daughter.'

'Katrina is my patient. I'll be doing the operation,' Sophie said. 'But if Charlie did it, she'd be in excellent hands. He's the director of surgery. He got the post because he's an excellent surgeon. And the papers whip up all that stuff about him to sell copies, so don't believe what you read. I'll come and see you immediately after the operation,' she said, and started moving the trolley out of the emergency department.

'Thank you for the vote of confidence,' Charlie said as they went into Theatre.

'It's the official line, isn't it?'

So she hadn't meant it. Not personally. 'Yeah,' he said, trying to ignore the sinking disappointment in the pit of his stomach. Why should it matter what she thought of him?

Though it did.

'It stopped the discussion. That's the main thing. Where's Sammy?' she asked the scrub nurse, wanting to know where her senior house officer was.

'Held up.'

'I'll assist,' Charlie said as Sophie started to scrub up. 'I was planning to observe all the surgeons anyway, so I may as well kill two birds with one stone.'

'Observe?' Sophie asked coolly.

'I need to know my team's capabilities. Where your strengths are, how you do things, where we can learn from each other.'

'So, despite what you said to me, you *are* planning new-broom stuff.'

'No.' He kept his temper under wraps. Just. Hadn't they

agreed on a truce last week? And he'd thought they'd been getting on all right, before they'd seen the Jacksons. Obviously he'd been wrong. 'But I believe in keeping my team motivated. To do that, I need to know where you are now and where you want to be. And it's my job to get you the extra experience you need to move your career onwards.'

As soon as Sophie had opened Katrina's abdomen and suctioned out the blood, she groaned. 'Her spleen's split completely in two. Gluing isn't an option.' She nodded at the screen where Katrina's spleen was visible.

'Agreed. It's going to have to come out,' Charlie said.

'Her BP's dropping,' the anaesthetist said.

'OK. I want four units of O-negative on standby, please. In the meantime, we need to filter and reuse her blood,' Sophie said. 'I'm doing an open operation, not laparoscopic,' she added to Charlie. 'Do I need to explain my decisions to you?'

'Later. Just do it,' Charlie said.

Sophie increased the size of her incision so she could perform the operation. To her relief, there were no further complications and the rest of the operation was textbook—grasping the splenic pedicle between the fingers of one hand, ligating the splenic artery, splenic vein and short gastric arteries, then removing the spleen, while trying not to damage the tail of the pancreas or the splenic flexure of the colon.

'Would you like to close?' she asked Charlie.

'As I'm assisting?'

'As your suturing is neater than mine,' she corrected.

Was that the ghost of a smile in her eyes? Or her idea of an olive branch? Whatever. He nodded and stitched the wound.

'How is she?' Derek asked, as soon as Sophie came out of Theatre.

'Her spleen had completely split in two,' Sophie said. 'I'm afraid I had to remove it. The good news is that Katrina should come round from the anaesthetic in a few minutes, and you'll be able to see her then. She'll be a bit wobbly at first, but she'll be fine. She'll be transferred to the paediatric ward, and she'll be in for a week or so. She'll have a drip to get fluids into her system and help with pain relief, and the stitches will dissolve by themselves so she won't have to have them removed.'

'What does the spleen do?' Alice asked.

'It filters the blood and helps fight infection,' Charlie explained. 'Katrina will be fine without a spleen, but it does mean that she's more likely to get an infection.' There was one thing that worried him: some Jehovah's Witnesses had issues with injections. If Katrina's family shared those beliefs, too, that could be a problem. 'Has she had the Hib immunisation?'

'Yes,' Alice said.

'Good.' And better than he'd expected. 'The Hib bacteria—haemophilus influenza type B—is the most common problem, but as she's been immunised she should be fine,' Sophie said. 'You need to watch that she doesn't get bitten by an animal—she's more likely to develop an infection afterwards. We'll also give you a card she needs to carry around with her which will tell any other medics that she has no spleen, or you could get her to wear a medical alert bracelet. And she'll need antibiotics before she has any dental work done to avoid the risk of her getting sepsis. The staff on the paediatric ward will be able to reassure you about her care, or you're welcome to contact me if you have any questions.'

'Did you —?' Alice began.

Derek placed his hand warningly on his wife's shoulder. 'Don't ask. Then you can honestly say that to your knowledge the answer is no.'

'But—'

'Actually, no. I won't lie to you—I did have blood on standby. If the worst had happened, I would have had to act very, very quickly to save Katrina's life. But we managed with autologous transfusion and I'm going to give Katrina some plasma expander. She's going to be fine,' Sophie said gently. 'If you'd like to wait here in the relatives' room, I'll make sure the nursing staff come and get you as soon as she wakes up.'

'Thank you,' Derek said.

'While we're waiting for Katrina to come round, how about a bacon sandwich?' Charlie asked when they'd left the relatives' room.

'No, thanks. I have paperwork to do.'

'Scared?' he asked.

She lifted her chin. 'Why would I be?'

'Because,' he said mildly, 'I've noticed that you avoid me as much as possible. Even though we agreed on a truce.'

'I am *not* scared of you.'

'It's only a sandwich. And a coffee,' he said. 'Platonic. And to say thanks for the vote of confidence.'

She frowned. 'What do you mean?'

'As you said, it's the official party line. I was hired for my skill, not my title. I don't think you meant it, but you still didn't have to say it. Besides, I want to talk to you.'

'About what?'

'Your career plans. You're a good surgeon. You're precise, you tell the theatre staff what you need without being dictatorial or arrogant, and you'll make an excellent consultant. When you learn to take the emotion out of it.'

Her eyes widened. 'What emotion?'

'Your initial reactions to Alice Jackson. You played a very risky game with your divide-and-rule strategy.'

'You went along with it.'

'Against my own judgement. And it didn't work anyway,' he reminded her. 'Alice guessed what you were doing.'

'So what are you saying?'

'You have a cool head. You need a cool heart as well.'

'Sorry. I have red blood.'

'And a head full of prejudice. You're right. Forget the sandwich,' he said, and walked away. Before his own red blood fired into life and he did something stupid—like kissing her to break down the barriers between them.

CHAPTER FIVE

'WHAT's her name?' Seb asked.

'What are you talking about?' Charlie asked, feigning ignorance.

'You're distracted. That means a woman's involved. Not that I've seen any pictures in the gossip rags for a while, so you've managed to keep this one quiet.' Seb swirled the wine round in his glass and inhaled. 'Mmm. I love Margaux. And this is a good one, Charlie. I hope you took it from the cellars at Weston.'

'I took a case last time I was there,' Charlie admitted.

Seb grinned. 'Good. I don't see why Barry should get all the benefits from Dad's cellar. Especially as, strictly speaking, it's *your* cellar.' He gave his brother a sidelong look. 'Don't tell me. She's tall, blonde and pretty.'

Charlie sighed. 'Medium height, blonde and pretty, actually. And nothing's going to happen because, unlike some people around here, I don't play around at home.'

Seb pounced. 'Aha. So you work with her. Nurse?'

'No, but it's irrelevant.'

'Charlie, Charlie, Charlie.' Seb shook his head sadly. 'You can't go looking for another Julia for ever.'

'I am *not* looking for another Julia,' Charlie said, stung.

'Then why do you always go for blondes?'

'I don't.'

Seb snorted. 'Yes, you do. And Vic agrees with me.'

When would his younger siblings stop trying to run his life? Charlie gritted his teeth. 'Leave it, Seb. I told you, nothing's going to happen.'

'Not a nurse. Fellow surgeon, then? Hmm.' Seb cut himself a slice of Stilton. 'Well, at least you picked one with brains this time. And, since she's a doctor, she has strong moral values—yes?'

Remembering the Jacksons, Charlie nodded. Sophie had strong moral values, unlike his ex-fiancée. On the other hand, she'd bent the rules about ethics. Even though her motives had been pure—to keep her patient safe—she hadn't played entirely by the rules. Which was another reason why he ought to stay away from her. 'Seb, if you want to interfere in someone's love life, why don't you pick on Vicky?'

Seb gave Charlie his most charming smile. 'Because she'd skin me?'

'I could skin you. I have scalpels.' Charlie rubbed his face thoughtfully. 'Actually, out of the two of us, I do the most work with skin. By a long, long way.'

'Ah, but you're a soft touch. Push comes to shove, you wouldn't use them on me,' Seb said with a grin. 'Why don't you go for it? You need a good woman. It stops things getting...pent up.'

Charlie scowled at his younger brother. 'Don't be crude.'

'I can be cruder than that.' Seb raised an eyebrow. 'Dish the dirt, brother mine. Unless you want me to leave it for Vic to ferret out?'

And their sister definitely wouldn't take no for an answer. Charlie sighed. 'Have I told you how much I hate you?'

'Frequently.' Seb topped up their glasses. 'Kid brothers are meant to be annoying. You can tell me, or you can tell Vic. Your choice.'

Charlie leaned back in his chair. 'OK. She's serious, clever—and she doesn't like me very much.'

'What's not to like about you?' Seb's eyes glittered.

'Drop the she-wolf act, Seb. You're the wrong sex.'

Seb lifted his chin, looking every inch the aristocrat. '*Nobody* disses my brother,' he said, his accent pure cut-glass.

'She hasn't dissed me.' Well, not straight out. Charlie sighed. 'She just…avoids me most of the time. I think it's because of my title.'

Seb snorted. 'That's tactics, bro. Reverse psychology. She's just playing hard to get in the hope that you'll go running after her. Come on, you know women go weak at the knees at the thought of dating Baron Radley. Even more so when they find out he's not old or short with bad teeth and nasal hair. You're a prime catch—the reason half those celeb mags are still going.'

'They'd get much more gossip if they followed you. A different woman every night.'

'You go out with a different one every time,' Seb pointed out.

'I escort different people to different events, yes—but *I* don't sleep with them all.'

'That's your problem.' Seb grinned. 'Love's sweetest part, variety. And don't change the subject. What's she like?'

'She cares about her patients. And she's very close to her family—they took on second jobs to put her through med school.' And Charlie still envied her that. What would it be like to have parents who loved you enough to make your dreams come true? A mother who fussed over you and went pink with pride, instead of one who moaned that you should settle down and produce an heir—and then, when she realised that meant you'd need the family home back, started complaining about the limitations of the Dower House?

Though it seemed his brother had a different take on it. 'She's poor? Then, as I said before, reverse psychology,' Seb announced, digging into the cheeseboard again. 'Classic tactics. You pretend to despise money, when you really want it more than anything else.'

Charlie rolled his eyes. 'I don't *have* any money.'

'You would have if you made Barry-the-wannabe-baron pull his weight.'

'The estate isn't his problem. It's mine.'

'And it doesn't help that you let him and Mum live there rent-free. You even pay all their bills, for heaven's sake.' Seb shook his head in despair. 'I keep telling you, you're a soft touch, Charlie.'

'I'm not. How could I charge my own mother rent?'

Seb spread his hands. 'Business. I would. So would Vic.'

'Only because you both hate Barry.' And they resented their mother even more than he did. 'Look, I promised Dad I'd take care of her. I don't break my promises.'

'That's true. But you expect other people to be the same as you. And you always get disappointed.' The sparkle in Seb's eyes dimmed for a moment. 'Ah, live in the real world, Charlie. Find yourself a good woman who understands the score. No commitments.'

'You're the expert in that department,' Charlie said wryly. 'Let's just agree to differ, shall we?'

'As long as you watch your back. This woman of yours— who has a name, I take it?' When Charlie didn't answer, Seb continued, 'Whoever she is, my guess is she's a gold-digger. And I'm a better judge of character than you are.'

'You're just a cynic.'

'I'm a realist,' Seb said softly. 'Which is why I don't get hurt.'

Charlie had no answer to that. He'd already been hurt in the worst possible way by Julia. Although he was absolutely sure that Sophie wasn't another Julia.

'Seriously—women apart—are you happy at the Hampstead General?'

Charlie was relieved at the change of subject. 'I think so. I like the team, and there's good communication between the departments.' He wrinkled his nose. 'I'll have a battle on my hands with the budget.'

'Which you'll win,' Seb said confidently. 'You've had enough practice.'

With the estate. 'Yeah.'

Seb lifted his glass. 'Well, here's to my brother. Director of Surgery.' He grinned. 'Which means I have to get promoted in one year, eleven months and three weeks to keep on your tail.'

'Seb, you're such a wheeler-dealer, I'm surprised you haven't got the job already,' Charlie said.

Seb winked. 'I'm working on it. Mind you, I reckon Vic might beat us both. Our sister, the brain surgeon. Who works even more hours than you do.' He sighed. 'That's why I date so much, you know. To keep our joint average up. You two are such slackers.'

Charlie laughed. 'Yeah, right. But keep your nose out of my love life, Seb. I'm fine as I am.'

'OK. You've got a reprieve. Until next week,' Seb said. 'And then I'm setting Vic on you.'

Charlie topped up their glasses. 'Vic will side with me because I'm her favourite.'

'You *wish*,' Seb said, laughing. 'Hey, better cut yourself some of that Stilton before I scoff the lot...'

* * *

'Why is it, every time I see you, you have your nose in a journal?' Abby asked.

Sophie looked up and smiled at the younger doctor. 'Just keeping up to date.'

'Are you OK?'

Sophie frowned. 'Sure. Why?'

'Just…you've been a bit quiet lately, and you've bowed out of every social event, which isn't like you. You're normally right in the thick of it—in fact, you normally organise things. But you didn't go to see that new romantic comedy with us last night, you made some excuse not to go on the team curry night—*and* you didn't turn up to Charlie's drinks.'

Sophie waved a dismissive hand. 'I'm fine, Abby. Don't worry about me. How's it going with you know who?'

Abby folded her arms. 'Stop trying to change the subject. What's up, Soph?'

'Nothing.' Nothing she wanted to discuss, anyway.

Abby's eyes narrowed. 'It's not the unthinkable, is it? You're not secretly in love with someone?'

Sophie's smile was genuine this time. 'You sound just like my mum. No. I'm not in love.' Though there was someone she couldn't quite get out of her head. A pair of very, very blue eyes. A mouth that positively begged for a kiss. And he was the most unsuitable man she could have picked. They had nothing in common, she despised everything he stood for, and…

There was the rub. Despite everything, she was attracted to Charlie. Extremely attracted to him. And because she'd tried to deny it to herself, she'd been unfair to him. She'd rebuffed every overture of friendship he'd made.

Abby looked worried. 'You don't have a thing about Guy, do you?'

'Guy?' Abby thought she was in love with *Guy?* Sophie blinked hard. 'Where did that come from? I like him, a lot—but that's as far as it goes. Considering I've been trying to fix you up with him…' She spread her hands. 'What on earth makes you think I've got the hots for Guy?'

'It's just he hasn't really noticed me. And with you being a bit—well, not yourself—I wondered…'

'No. Definitely not Guy,' Sophie reassured her with a grin.

'Who, then?'

She'd rather eat worms than admit that to anyone. Sophie sighed. 'Abby, the only thing I'm interested in is my career. End of story.' She smiled to soften the harshness of her words. 'So how's your day been?'

'Brilliant. Charlie let me observe him in Theatre this morning—*and* he let me do some suturing again. He showed me how to do a couple of different knots, too. He's such a nice bloke.'

Yeah. And Sophie had been seriously unfair to him. She'd judged him by the standard of the people she'd known as a student. Just because he was upper class. Worse, he'd even told her that he had to work twice as hard as anyone else if he wanted people to take him seriously.

The next time she saw him she'd make amends, she promised herself.

And then her bleep went. She glanced at the display on her pager. Paeds. Emergency appendicectomy.

'Anyone needs me, I'm in Theatre Four,' she told Abby. 'Would you be an angel and stick it on the board for me?' The noticeboard in the department told everyone where the surgeons were.

'Will do.'

Sophie made her way to Theatre, scrubbed swiftly and

was briefed on the case. Over two thirds of children admitted to hospital with suspected appendicitis turned out to have a completely different condition. If the patient didn't have the classic signs of acute appendicitis, they were kept in for observation until the symptoms settled or the diagnosis became clear. It was more difficult to diagnose abdominal tenderness in children, and most of the tests were unreliable—although asking the child to stand and hop on their right leg was one of the better ones. If they could do it, it was unlikely that they had any peritoneal tenderness.

'The house officer thought it was a urinary tract infection,' Angus McFadden, the paediatrician, told her in Theatre as he did the handover.

'Could've been. Or pancreatitis. Or something rarer— Meckel's diverticulum, which you can only distinguish from appendicitis by a laparotomy,' Sophie pointed out. 'We all had to learn, once.'

'Yes.' McFadden's eyes hardened slightly when he clearly realised that Sophie wasn't going to join him in moaning about how useless junior doctors were nowadays.

'Is your house officer here? It might be useful experience to see the appendicectomy,' Sophie suggested.

McFadden looked daggers at her; she smiled back at him. 'I don't mind an audience.'

As she'd hoped, he was concerned enough about appearances to ring down to Paediatrics and order his house officer up.

'Sophie Harrison, general surgeon,' she introduced herself when the house officer walked in, looking nervous.

'Aidan Merrick,' he said.

'Nice to meet you, Aidan. I could have done this by laparotomy, but I think there's a risk of the appendix bursting, so I'm doing an open operation. I've done a Lanz incision—that's the low skin crease incision—because it gives a better cosmetic result than the higher one centred on McBurney's point. I've opened the layers of the abdominal wall along their fibres—and I've just lifted the peritoneum. There was some watery fluid and pus there, so I've sent a sample off for culture. I'm just feeling for the appendix here—it's definitely inflamed, because it's sticking, so I'm going to dissect it out rather than just push it out with my finger.' She talked Aidan through the rest of the operation, explaining what she was doing and why, and showing Aidan how the area around the appendix was thick and friable. She ligated the blood supply, crushed the appendix base and tied absorbable sutures before removing it, then guided a sump-sucker into the pelvis with her finger to suck out the remaining pus and fluid. Finally, she swabbed the area with gauze to remove any remaining pus and minimise the risk of the little girl developing a pelvic infection or abscess.

'I'm using absorbable sutures for the deeper layers, but I'm leaving the skin open because there was infection,' she explained.

When they'd finished, Aidan made a point of staying behind in the scrubs room. 'I just wanted to say thanks—for not biting my head off, and for giving me the chance to see the op.'

'Pleasure. And I don't bite people's heads off unless they make the same mistake twice, or try to cover it up,' Sophie said. 'We've all been house officers.'

'Not if you talk to McF—' He stopped abruptly. 'Sorry. I shouldn't have said that.'

'I didn't hear you say anything.' Sophie smiled at him. 'If it helps, I remember my first year as a qualified doctor. I spent most of the time being terrified I'd do something wrong, or tired because I'd been on call for so many hours. And sometimes your superiors forget what it was like to be a junior doctor. Hang on in there.'

'Thanks.' He shuffled his feet. 'Um, I wondered if you'd like to go for a drink or something? If you're not busy, that is.'

Uh-oh. Was that the beginnings of hero-worship she could see in his eyes? Not good. And she didn't need romantic entanglements to complicate her life. Better make him understand her actions hadn't been motivated by personal feelings but by a principle. 'It's very sweet of you to ask,' Sophie said gently, 'but there's no need. I would've stood up for anyone in your position.'

'Oh.' He looked embarrassed.

She smiled at him again. 'See you around.'

'Right.' He took the hint and left the room. Sophie finished changing. She was on her way into her office to collect her things when she saw Charlie walking towards her.

'I've just seen Angus McFadden,' he greeted her.

'Oh.' It hadn't even occurred to her that McFadden would make a complaint. Obviously he had. And quickly, too. Well, she'd deal with it. 'Is there a problem?' she asked, lifting her chin and giving him her coolest, most professional gaze.

He gave her a wry smile. 'Only with his ego.'

She blinked. Was she hearing things?

'We had a little chat. I explained to him that my staff believe in supporting junior doctors and giving them a chance to learn. And I agree with them absolutely.'

McFadden had complained about her and Charlie had backed her? The rush of pleasure was followed by an even stronger rush of guilt. She really *had* been unfair to him. He would have been quite within his rights to tear strips off her for not obeying protocol and questioning the judgement of a senior doctor in a different speciality. 'Thank you.' He looked tired, she thought. There were definite dark smudges underneath his eyes, and his skin looked washed out. 'Are you OK?' she asked.

He shrugged. 'Just finished dealing with a burns case. Don't get me started on the subject of people mistreating their stepchildren.'

That sounded as if it went a bit deeper than the usual doctor's railing against inadequate parenting. Something *personal*. She linked her fingers behind her back to stop herself impulsively hugging him. Something told her that Charlie wouldn't appreciate her guessing that something had hurt him or speculating what the problem was.

'My mum always says a decent meal makes you feel a bit better. Tell you what, I'll shout you a fry-up at the local greasy spoon,' she offered.

'Thanks, but I'll pass.'

She tried to suppress a little stab of hurt. What had she expected? After the way she'd acted towards him, it was hardly surprising that he didn't want to spend time with her.

'Not that I don't want to,' he said, as if reading her face. 'Just that I tend to be…' He paused, as if searching for the right word. 'Hassled, when I'm out. It's just easier not to go.'

'Sure.'

Was it her imagination, or was there some weird kind of tension in the corridor? Something that was pulling them closer? She started to suggest that they go to the hospital canteen instead, when she realised he was speaking.

'Sorry. You, first,' she said.

'I was going to say, if you're heading home, I might walk with you—if you don't mind.'

She frowned. 'We might not live in the same direction.'

Charlie shrugged. 'I just need a walk to clear my head.'

She knew that feeling. A bad day in Theatre—one where you lost your patient, or you had a domestic violence case where the patient claimed it was clumsiness, and you knew that you'd just patched up your patient for now and you'd be doing exactly the same thing for the same patient in a few weeks' time. The kind of day where, at the end of it, you wanted to be alone—and yet you didn't want to be alone either. 'OK. Here's the deal. How about you walk me home and I make you dinner?'

He narrowed his eyes, as if he wasn't sure he'd heard her correctly.

'Nothing fancy,' she added. 'Probably just pasta. Depends what's in my fridge.'

'Pasta,' he said softly, 'sounds just about perfect.'

'Good. I'll just get my stuff.'

He nodded. 'Meet you back here in ten minutes?'

'Ten minutes is fine.'

'And, Sophie?'

'Hmm?' She looked back over her shoulder at him.

'Thank you,' he said softly.

CHAPTER SIX

To Charlie's surprise, Sophie was already in the corridor when he came back from his office. Then again, Sophie Harrison wasn't like any other woman he'd ever met. Except maybe Vicky. She had that same kind of seriousness about her. Although his feelings towards Sophie definitely weren't fraternal—and he didn't really want to analyse how he did feel where Sophie was concerned. They were hardly even friends. They barely knew each other. But he was drawn to her.

A moth to a flame.

Bad move. He should make some excuse and just go home. On his own.

Except his mouth refused to frame the words.

They walked together in silence through the back streets to Sophie's flat. It was an easy silence. She seemed to understand he wasn't in the mood to make small talk. That he didn't want to be alone—but he didn't want to share the load in his head either. Sensitive. He appreciated that.

As they walked along, his hand brushed against hers. Just once. It was as if some kind of current flowed between them—just in time, he folded his fingers into his palm. Her offer of dinner meant food. It didn't mean she wanted him to hold her hand.

Maybe this was a bad move. Sophie made him feel like a

hormonal teenager. She was a colleague. Well, technically, he was her boss, so that meant hands off. And he wasn't in the market for a relationship anyway. He had too much baggage to carry around. Weston, the estate, heirs—ah, hell. All he wanted to be was a doctor. Why couldn't life be *simple?* Why couldn't he have been born someone else?

Sophie unlocked the door to a shared lobby, then unlocked another door and stood aside. 'It's straight up the stairs,' she said.

'It's convenient for work,' he said. They weren't far from the hospital.

'I know—it's walking distance. I was lucky to get it. But my landlady—who lives on the ground floor—has a soft spot for doctors. Plus I feed her cat while she's away. She leaves her key with me.' Sophie grinned. 'Mind you, if she pops round when my mum's here, you can't get a word in edge-ways between the two of them.'

He stifled a ripple of envy. When had his mother last vis-ited his flat? Though maybe that was his own fault. Given the choice between having his mother and Barry using his place as a hotel and paying for them to stay somewhere on their rare trips to London, he'd opted to keep his privacy.

Sophie's flat, although immaculately tidy, felt warm and inviting. The kind of place where people would congregate. And, judging from the photographs pinned on a cork board in her kitchen, people congregated around Sophie a lot. Some of the pictures were of hospital staff, on what he assumed were departmental nights out of some sort. Others were of people he didn't know, but some of them bore a close resemblance to Sophie. Family, he guessed, and his stomach tightened.

'Why the thaw?' he asked, needing to know.

'Thaw?' She switched the kettle on.

'We didn't exactly get off to a good start.' She'd made it

very clear she didn't like him. 'But you invited me here to dinner tonight.'

'You walked me home.'

He didn't buy that. And obviously it showed on his face, because she shrugged. 'OK. I suppose I felt a bit guilty. I haven't really given you a chance since you started at the Hampstead General.'

He waited for her to tell him why.

As he'd hoped, she filled the silence. 'I assumed you'd be like the upper-class—' She stopped, as if biting something back, then continued quietly, 'Like the med students I knew. And you're not.'

So she'd had a hard time at med school because of her background? He could see how that would make her dislike people from the so-called privileged classes. Although maybe it was time she let go of old grudges. 'Most eighteen-year-old boys have a lot of growing up to do,' he said quietly. 'And most first-year students are a pain in the neck.'

She knew that, but the students concerned hadn't been first years. Far from it. It had happened in her final year, and—Sophie stopped herself. She wasn't going to think about that. And she definitely wasn't going to tell Charlie what had happened. It was none of his business. 'Do you take sugar in your coffee?'

'No, just milk, thanks.' He nodded to the gossip magazine in the middle of the table. *Celebrity Life.* 'Do you actually read these things?'

'No, it's my mum's. She's a sucker for those TV programmes where celebs show you around their homes, too.' Sophie pulled a face. 'Not my style at all.'

He didn't say a word, but she could see on his face that he didn't believe her. What was his problem? Did he think all the have-nots wanted to see how the rich and famous lived? Well, she didn't give a damn about money or fame. They weren't important. It was who you were and how you behaved towards others that counted. And people of Charlie's class forgot that way too often, in her view.

'For your information, my mum never carries any paper on her. So when she wants to leave me a message, she scribbles one on the front of whatever magazine she happens to be reading at the time.' Sophie lifted her chin. 'We were supposed to have lunch tomorrow as I've got a half-day. But Mum obviously got the wrong day and popped over today. She's the queen of scattiness.'

And mine's the queen of ice, Charlie thought. Or maybe women were just like that around him. Sophie certainly seemed to be freezing on him, and he had no idea what he'd said to upset her. All he'd done had been to ask about the gossip rag on the table. What had been the harm in that?

'Look, I wasn't questioning you. It's up to you what you read. Or not,' he added hastily as he saw her eyes harden.

Sophie picked up the magazine and read the handwritten message on the paler parts of the photograph on the front cover. A smile softened her face. 'Oh, *yes!*'

'What?' Charlie asked.

'She's left me a cake. Which means we have pudding. And my mum makes the best cake in the world.'

Something that should be patented, if it could turn someone's mood from ice to sunshine at the mere mention of it—but Charlie kept that thought to himself. He didn't want any more misunderstandings between them.

She dropped the magazine on the worktop, finished making the coffee and handed him a mug. 'Don't stand on ceremony. Grab a chair and I'll fix us some food.'

'Can I do anything to help?'

'No, it's fine. Just chill. If you're really bored, there are some medical journals in my living room.'

'I'm all right here.' Too tired to move, really. His last case in Theatre had left him drained. Sick. How could somebody deliberately burn another person? Particularly when that other person was so much smaller. Surely children should be protected *by* their parents, not *from* them?

Though cruelty could take other forms than physical hurt. Emotional neglect, for starters.

But he wasn't going to think about that now. Not here.

This was the last place he'd expected to find himself. Sitting in Sophie Harrison's kitchen, watching her make pasta sauce. She was as precise in the kitchen as she was in the operating theatre, he thought as he watched her chop onions, garlic and mushrooms. She didn't measure anything, he noticed as she tipped a large glug of red wine into the pot. And she worked fast. Somehow there was bread baking in the oven and pasta on the boil and, for the first time in a long, long while, Charlie felt at home. At peace. He could sit here for ages, just watching Sophie. There was something soothing about her. Balm to his soul.

She brought heaped plates over to the table and added a plate of hot crusty bread and a tub of butter. 'Are you on call tonight?'

'No.'

'Me neither.' She poured two glasses of red wine and handed him one. 'Sorry it's nothing fancy.'

'I don't eat cordon bleu and drink vintage wine every day of the week, you know.' He grimaced and rubbed a hand over his eyes as he saw the hurt in her face. 'Sorry, sorry. I didn't mean to snap at you.'

'And I wasn't implying anything either—it's just a scratch meal.' She shrugged. 'If I'd *planned* to cook you something, it would've been a bit more interesting. That's all I meant.'

'This,' Charlie said honestly, 'looks wonderful.' After the first mouthful he revised his opinion. 'And tastes even better.'

'Not quite up to my mum's standard but, hey.' She grinned. 'Not that she ever sticks to a recipe book. She changes things as she goes along. I learned at her knee, so I tend to make things up as I go along, too.'

Charlie couldn't ever remember his mother cooking. They'd always had a cook. They still did, although his mother wasn't the one who paid her wages. 'It sounds as if you had a happy childhood.' Lucky, lucky Sophie. He'd have given a great deal for that.

She nodded. 'I did—and even though I am an only child, I'm part of a much bigger family. We still have a family Sunday once a month, but there are too many of us to make it a proper roast lunch and fancy tea like it was when I was a kid. We just pile round to my mum's and all take something with us, a pot-luck thing. Summer's even better, because my dad takes charge of the barbecue and my uncles set up a bouncy castle in the back garden for the kids.'

Something he'd never done. 'Sounds like fun,' he said wistfully.

'You'd hate it.'

'Why? Because I'm a baron?'

Sophie sighed. 'No. Because when my family's together and they've sunk a few beers, they're noisy. Actually, they're noisy even without the beers. Then there are all the kids running around—it's a bit chaotic. Not the kind of thing I imagine you're used to. I get the impression you're used to something a bit quieter and more refined.'

'It's not all it's cracked up to be, having a title. Sometimes I wish…' He stopped. Hell, why was he pouring his heart out to Sophie like this? He barely knew her.

'What?' she asked softly.

'Nothing. Just ignore me. It's been a rough day.'

'Heartstrings case, huh?'

He frowned. 'How do you mean?'

'The sort where you patch someone up and you know it's just going to happen again and again. And no matter how many phone calls you make, how many wheels you set in motion, you know it's not going to be enough to stop it happening. There's always an excuse—not enough funds, not enough staff, not enough time.'

'Yeah.'

To his surprise, she reached across the table and took his hand. 'Don't beat yourself up about it. You did what you could.'

'It wasn't enough. I gave the mother the number of a women's refuge, and she just screwed it up and threw it away.'

'But she knows it exists now. You've planted a seed. One day, it might grow.'

'When it might be too late. She's going to go back to her man. And that poor little kid… I alerted Social Services, but you can tell they're going to lie about it. An accident. Oh, the bath water was a bit too hot. The child must have done it himself. Hell, everyone knows you put the cold water in first and check the temperature before you let a kid anywhere near it!'

She squeezed his hand and released it. 'Last time I looked, saving the world wasn't in a surgeon's job description. Or is it different in plastics?'

'No.'

'Uh-huh. You all just *think* you're superheroes.'

There wasn't a bite to her words. He glanced up, met her gaze and realised that she was trying to tease him out of his mood. Unwillingly, he smiled. 'Something like that.'

She changed the conversation to something light and fluffy, and by the end of the meal he found himself laughing for real.

And then she gave him some cake.

'This is seriously good.' Although he'd eaten a large main course, Charlie wolfed down his cake.

She pushed the plate over towards him. 'Help yourself to some more.'

'Thanks. I will. It's gorgeous, but…' He frowned. 'I can't place the taste.'

'Coriander spice cake. It's made with porridge oats and yoghurt, so it's sort of good for you.'

Charlie scoffed. 'No way. Something that tastes this good has to be sinful. Addictive.'

And then he wished he hadn't said that. Because he could think of something else that would taste good. Something else that would be sinful. Addictive.

Sophie's mouth.

Thank God she wasn't able to read his mind, because she merely made them both another mug of coffee.

'Ready to talk about it yet?'

But they *had* talked about his patient. Or… He felt his eyes widen. She'd guessed there was more? 'Nothing to talk about.'

She gave him a disbelieving look, but to his relief she let it drop and allowed him to steer the conversation back to something trivial.

Before he realised it, it was ten o'clock. He stood up. 'Sorry. I've hogged your evening. And your cake. Let me wash up before I go.'

She shook her head. 'There isn't much to do. And you look bone-tired. Bed's the best place for you.'

His heart missed a beat. Bed?

Oh, ridiculous. She wasn't offering. She'd meant *his* bed. On his own.

Though he had to face it. He'd like to sleep in Sophie Harrison's bed. With her. And wake up with her. Make love with her in the quiet of a London dawn.

And if she had the slightest idea what was going on in his head right now, it would be goodbye to ever having a decent working relationship with her—let alone anything else.

'Is it OK if I call a taxi?' he asked.

'Sure. You live in completely the opposite direction, don't you?' she asked.

He nodded. 'But I needed the company tonight.'

'I normally call Z-cabs, if that's any help—they're only just down the road from here. Their card's next to the phone.' She nodded to the phone mounted on the wall next to the cork board.

'Thanks.' He made the call swiftly. 'They'll be five minutes,' he said.

'They're pretty good—they're usually on time.'

'I'd better wait for them downstairs.'

'Sure.'

'Thank you,' he said softly as they stood in the lobby a minute or two later.

'What for?'

'For letting me just…be.'

'Be yourself?' she guessed perceptively.

He nodded. 'Something like that. It doesn't happen very often.'

'Sounds as if you could do with a friend.'

Except the way he was feeling towards Sophie wasn't just

friendly. He knew he should leave. Now. But he couldn't. Not when her lips were slightly parted. Not when those beautiful brown eyes looked at him like that.

He couldn't stop himself. He bent his head and very gently brushed his mouth against hers. When she didn't pull back or slap him, he did it again. The next thing he knew, he'd loosened her hair and had threaded his fingers through it—soft, so soft. She felt like heaven—and his mouth was coaxing Sophie's lips to part even more.

And Sophie was starting to kiss him back.

Hell, he'd wanted this so much. Wanted to feel her body close to his, so close he could feel her heart beating. Wanted the warmth of her skin against his. Wanted her to kiss his demons away.

It couldn't happen. He had to stop.

Right now.

Except he couldn't. Not when it felt so good, so right, to hold her and kiss her. Time seemed to slow to the point where it didn't exist any more. All he was aware of was Sophie and the sweetness of her mouth.

The beep of a car horn shocked them apart.

He dragged in a breath. 'I'm sorry. I shouldn't have done that. I just…' Just couldn't help himself. Wanted to be a real person for once, instead of Charlie, Baron Radley. Wanted Sophie's warmth to enfold him.

'Don't worry. I won't be ringing *Celebrity Life* to give them a kiss-and-tell,' she said dryly.

He shook his head. 'That isn't what I meant. But we have to work together. I think it's best if we pretend we didn't just do that.'

'Sure.' Her face was completely unreadable. He couldn't look at her mouth—it would drive him crazy with longing, now he knew what she tasted like. Sweetness and spice. Like the cake she'd just fed him. And, oh, how he wanted more.

He just couldn't have it.

The taxi horn sounded again.

'I have to go. I'll, um, see you on the ward tomorrow. Thanks for dinner.'

'No worries.'

Cool, calm and collected. As if nothing had happened.

But it had, he thought as the taxi drove him back to his own flat. He knew what she felt like in his arms. He knew what it was like to kiss her.

But how could he ask her to be part of his life? She'd hate it. She'd hate the brittle social circle he moved in. She'd hate all the stupid protocol in his world. She'd hate having her privacy ripped away by the paparazzi—he'd been more than lucky tonight that no one had snapped him walking from the hospital with Sophie.

And then there was the whole mess of Weston, the baggage that dragged him down. The estate that needed a dynastic engagement. And the entailments that meant he couldn't give it up—though, even if he could, that would mean dumping the burdens on Seb or Vicky. No way could he drag them down like that.

And what the hell was he thinking anyway, wondering if she'd be part of his life? Today was the first time they'd been on more than wary keep-your-distance terms. She'd just cooked him dinner tonight and he'd kissed her—and he was planning happily-ever-afters? Talk about jumping the gun! But there was something about Sophie—something that made him get carried away. And he couldn't afford to do that. Not with Weston and all the rest of it to think about. He'd done the right thing, telling her to forget that kiss. But if only things were different.

'You look like you've got the world on your shoulders, mate,' the cabbie said when he pulled up outside Charlie's flat.

Sometimes, Charlie thought, it felt like it. 'I'm fine,' he lied, and paid the fare.

I think it's best if we pretend we didn't just do that.

The memory made Sophie cringe, and she took it out on the saucepan, scrubbing it a lot harder than was warranted.

It wasn't supposed to be like that. She'd felt guilty about the way she'd misjudged him. And he'd looked miserable and tired. She'd automatically suggested her mum's solution to the world's problems—a decent home-cooked meal and a bit of space to talk. It was what she'd have done for any of her other colleagues.

Except she wouldn't have kissed any of her other colleagues.

Oh, this was bad. Embarrassing in the extreme. OK, so Charlie had been the one to start the kissing. He'd been the one to loosen her hair. But she'd kissed him back. And if that taxi hadn't beeped its horn…

She didn't want to think about what might have happened. What she might have admitted. That would have been too, too much.

It was bad enough as it was. Charlie probably thought she'd been coming on to him. And he'd called a halt—because she was too common for him.

Tomorrow, Sophie thought, was going to be hideous.

And she'd somehow have to brazen it out.

CHAPTER SEVEN

SOPHIE took a handful of body scrub, and wished that her thoughts could be sloughed away as easily as dead skin. Why the hell had she kissed Charlie back last night? After he'd gone, she'd tried to busy herself with medical journals and messing about on the Internet, but she'd ended up thinking about him. Worse, she'd *dreamed* about him. X-rated dreams. Dreams about being naked with him. Feeling his hard, muscular body drive into hers.

This was bad. She hadn't felt like that about anyone in a long, long time.

Since she'd been a student. Since that night.

She rubbed the scrub harder into her skin. That night was buried and forgotten. In the past. End of story.

And it wasn't as if she hadn't had a boyfriend since. She'd had dates. But she'd been busy with her career, starting out as a junior doctor and working her way up the ladder—putting the hours in, learning everything she could—and she hadn't had time for a love life. Frankly, she liked her life as it was. A busy working life and a good social life, with all the hugs and platonic kisses she needed from her friends and family. So she just had to push Charlie out of her head. Push that kiss out of her head. It was never going to work between them: his family were practically royalty, and hers were plain old East End.

So. They were colleagues only. And it had only been one little kiss. And one little kiss wasn't going to turn her whole world upside down, was it? She was too strong, too sensible, to let that happen.

But she was very, very glad she was only on a half-day shift today. With any luck, she'd have finished the ward rounds and be in Theatre before she bumped into Charlie—and with even more luck, she'd be out of Theatre and off duty before he'd finished his list.

Between breakfast and walking to work, she texted her mother to confirm lunch. And then it was time to face the ward. And Charlie.

Nobody gave her strange looks when she walked in. Nobody asked her any awkward questions. It was just as if last night hadn't happened. The hospital grapevine wasn't whispering a thing.

Good.

Her ward round was uneventful—to her relief, no sign of Charlie—and then her bleep went. She glanced at the display and rang the emergency department. 'Sophie Harrison. You paged me?'

'Soph, it's Paul. We've got an icky one for you. Toddler swallowed a couple of his gran's hearing-aid batteries.'

'Ouch.' Usually, if a child swallowed a foreign body and wasn't in pain, and the X-rays showed that the object had passed through the upper end of the oesophagus, they waited for it to pass through the child's system naturally. But hearing-aid batteries were too dangerous to leave—they were likely to disintegrate in the child's throat or stomach and release toxic mercury salts, leading to tissue death or perforation around the area of the battery. 'Have you done an X-ray?'

'Yep, and it's in the oesophagus. It hasn't gone down as far as the bronchial tree. And, before you ask, we've kept the child nil by mouth—according to his grandmother, he hasn't had anything to drink since before breakfast.'

Which was one of the signs of an ingested foreign body: refusal to drink, difficulty in breathing and excess saliva, sometimes with black flecks in it if the child had swallowed a battery.

'Any idea how long ago it happened?'

'About three hours, as far as I can make out.'

Good. A child needed to be nil by mouth for at least two hours before an endoscopy.

'I don't think we're going to be able to remove it with a Foley catheter,' Paul added. 'So I put him on a glucose drip before I paged you.'

'Excellent. I'll alert Theatre and see you downstairs in a minute,' Sophie said.

She checked the X-rays in ED. There was a two-step ring—clearly a battery and not a coin—in the child's oesophagus. Exactly where she'd expected it: the cricopharyngeous sling at C6, where around seventy per cent of foreign bodies were caught.

'What we're going to do is something called an endoscopy,' she explained to the little boy's grandmother. 'It's a flexible tube with a camera on the end—it goes down your throat and lets me see what's going on. I'll be able to see where the battery is and take it out.'

'It's an operation?' she asked, clearly upset.

Sophie nodded. 'We can do the procedure under sedation, so he's awake when we do it, but it's complicated in really little ones and they need much higher doses of sedation than older ones. I'd be happier doing it under a general anaesthetic.'

'My daughter's going to be so angry with me. I only turned my back for a second. I didn't think he'd go rummaging in my bedroom drawer!'

'Nobody's blaming you,' Sophie soothed her. 'It's really common in this age group. The under-twos put everything in their mouths.'

'I was supposed to be looking after him while my daughter was at a job interview. I couldn't phone her, not when she was about to go in for the interview.'

'Of course not. You did the right thing, bringing him here,' Sophie said. 'If you'd like to wait in the relatives' room, I'll come in to see you as soon as we're out of Theatre and he's woken up.'

'But she'll ring me when she comes out. She'll panic when I don't answer.'

'Does she have a mobile phone?' Sophie asked.

'Yes. I've got the number in my diary.'

'Then as soon as you think she'll be out of the interview, one of the nurses will ring her for you,' Sophie said with a smile. 'Don't worry. Everything's going to be fine.'

The procedure was a straightforward one, and when Sophie retrieved the battery she was relieved to see that it hadn't started disintegrating. They'd caught it early enough so the little boy was unlikely to have any burns on the inside of his throat. There were no complications with the anaesthesia either, and she was soon able to return to the relatives' room.

'He's absolutely fine,' she reassured the elderly woman. 'He can't have any milk or solids for the next six hours, and we'll keep him in for observation on the paediatric ward upstairs. But you can stop worrying now,' she said with a smile.

'Oh, thank God. I was so worried about him and I don't know how I would have faced my daughter if anything had happened to him. She'll never leave him with me again as it is.'

'Once she's got over the initial shock, I'm sure she'll come round,' Sophie soothed. 'It could have happened anywhere. Don't blame yourself.'

She finished the rest of her morning list. To her relief, there was no sign of Charlie. He was probably in a meeting or something. Relaxed, she opened the door to the ward—and Charlie was striding down the corridor towards her.

Her heart rate speeded up. He didn't have that hunted look about him, the one that had made her want to comfort him last night. Instead, his face was absolutely unreadable.

'Good afternoon,' she said.

He nodded. 'OK?'

'Sure.'

Anyone listening wouldn't have a clue that he'd kissed her last night. That he'd loosened her hair. That the only reason they'd stopped had been because his taxi had arrived.

He really was good at this 'pretending nothing had happened' bit. Or maybe that was what happened when you spent half your life in the public eye. You learned to put on an act.

'Half-day?'

'Yeah.'

'Enjoy it. Anything I need to know about?'

She shook her head. 'Everything's fine.'

'Good.'

And that was it. One quick smile—one she didn't think was quite genuine, because it didn't reach his eyes—and he was gone.

What had she expected? A declaration of undying love?

He'd said last night that they should pretend that kiss hadn't happened. And that was fine by her.

Then why was her lower lip tingling? Why did she feel flat, disappointed? Why did she feel this yearning to touch him again?

Because, Sophie Harrison, you're stupid, she told herself sharply. It's a complication you don't need. Forget it.

She was still distracted, even through lunch with her mum. And Fran picked up on it.

'Sophie, you haven't heard a single word I've said.'

'Course I have, Mum.'

Fran tutted and topped up their coffee mugs from the cafetière. 'I'm your mother. I *know* when you're not listening. What's up? Work?'

'Work's fine.'

Fran gave her a hopeful look. 'Boyfriend?'

'No.' Sophie rolled her eyes. 'Mum, I'm too busy for a boyfriend.'

'And you're a modern woman and you don't need anyone to look after you.' Fran sighed. 'I know, I know. You've told me enough times. But I'd like to see you settle down with someone who'll make you happy.'

'I *am* happy, Mum. And there's plenty of time before I have to settle down.'

'You're thirty-two, Soph. Leave it much longer, and you'll have a tough time if you decide to have babies.'

'I'm not maternal.'

Fran snorted. 'Right. Which is why all the littlies can't wait for their Aunty Sophie to turn up on a Sunday afternoon. And why you spend most of your time on the floor with them, playing games and reading stories. And why you get on the bouncy castle with them.' She gestured to Sophie's fridge.

'And why you've got all those paintings stuck to your fridge with magnets.'

Paintings they'd done especially for her at nursery and school. Busted. 'All right, so I like kids.' Sophie gave a rueful smile. 'Mum, I just haven't met the right man yet. I'll know when I meet him.'

Her smile faded as a picture formed in her mind. Blue eyes and a vulnerable mouth. *Charlie.* Well, he wasn't Mr Right, he was Baron Wrong. And she'd better remember that.

For the next week, Charlie was perfectly polite towards Sophie at work, but she could tell he'd put a barrier up. He didn't socialise much either, though she no longer thought it was because he was a snob who didn't want to mix with the lower classes. Not after that heartfelt admission about being hassled when he was out.

Part of her wanted to break through his reserve, but the more sensible part of her knew it would be a bad idea. Charlie wasn't the one who could heal the scars she kept hidden. And she had a feeling that he was covering up an emotional minefield, too. Not a good combination.

All she had to do was remind her body of that. And then she wouldn't get those flashbacks of the feel of his arms round her, the taste of his mouth on hers.

She was just reminding herself of that when she walked into the staffroom and saw a stranger sitting there.

'Hello. Are you lost?' she asked.

'Lost?' the woman echoed.

'This is the surgical team's staffroom. If you were looking for the relatives' room, I can take you there,' Sophie offered.

'Oh. No. I'm not waiting to see a patient.'

Something about the woman seemed familiar, though

Sophie had no idea who she was. Something about her voice, too. Odd. 'Sophie Harrison,' she said, holding out her hand. 'Are you new to the team?'

The woman's handshake was firm, Sophie noted. Strong.

'No. I'm waiting for Charlie. My brother,' she explained.

'Oh, so you must be Vicky, the brain surgeon.' And that explained why the woman looked familiar. Sophie could see the family resemblance now—the same blue eyes and haughty features—though in Vicky they were softened slightly.

And right now Vicky looked surprised. 'Charlie talked to you about me?'

Sophie nodded. 'Look, Dr Radley—or is that Miss?'

She waved a hand. 'Vicky's easier.'

'Vicky. I think Charlie's off today.'

'No, he's definitely working...' Vicky frowned. 'Ah. Wrong place.'

Sophie frowned, too. 'No, he does work here.'

'But not on his days off. He's at Harley Street,' Vicky said.

Harley Street? Charlie was working in Harley Street?

Then all his talk about wanting to be like any other doctor was just a lie.

Harley Street was full of private clinics, and Charlie was a plastic surgeon. So his claims about not being a nip-and-tuck merchant weren't strictly true, were they? On his days off from the National Health Service, he was working in Harley Street. Earning shedloads of cash from the rich and famous, people who wanted their lips made pouty or their cleavage enhanced or their lined faces made youthful again. And in the meantime, those who couldn't pay for operations they really needed—operations that weren't just for vanity—just had to wait and wait and wait. 'I see,' Sophie said coldly.

'Actually, I don't think you do,' Vicky said.

'It's obvious. He's just playing at being a doctor here, and he's doing face lifts in Harley Street to rake in the money,' Sophie said, curling her lip in disgust.

'Firstly, Charlie's not the family playboy. That's Seb,' Vicky said. 'Secondly, Charlie's not doing face lifts.' She looked uncomfortable. 'And it's sort of not private work either.'

Sophie frowned. 'I'm not with you.'

'He doesn't charge for it. He blags the cost of theatre time from people he knows—they give it to him because it means they can say that Baron Radley works at their clinic—and he does paediatrics. Plastics work for kids whose parents can't afford to go private, but the waiting lists are so long that the kids are having to live in misery. He specialises in burns and tendon repair.'

Sophie blinked. 'I had no idea.'

'He keeps it to himself.' Vicky shrugged. 'Can you imagine what the press would make of it? Headlines everywhere, and they'd hail him as a hero. Which he is—but he doesn't like to talk about it.'

'So why are you telling me?' Sophie asked. It'd be so easy for her to go to the press and spill the beans, if she chose. *Celebrity Life* would love a scoop like this. Why had Vicky handed her the ammunition?

'If you don't know,' Vicky said, 'there's not much point in me explaining.'

Colour whooshed into Sophie's face. Had Charlie talked to his sister about *her?* But she'd already learned that Charlie was a private man. And he was good at putting on a 'nothing ever happened' act. Look at the way he'd been towards her since that kiss.

'You didn't really come here to see Charlie. You came to check me out,' Sophie accused, her eyes narrowing.

Vicky shrugged. 'He's my brother. Someone has to look out for him.'

Sophie lifted her chin. 'Two things. Firstly, I might not be from your class, but I'm not a gold-digger. I don't give a toss about money or class. Secondly, Charlie is my colleague, and that's all.'

'My brother's very good at putting up smoke screens,' Vicky said thoughtfully. 'Seb and I are about the only ones who can see through them.'

'There's nothing going on between us.'

'No?' Vicky raised an eyebrow.

'No.'

Vicky grinned. 'I think I'm going to like you. We're on the same side.'

'What side?'

'Charlie's,' Vicky said simply. 'See you around.'

And before Sophie had the chance to say anything else, Vicky left the staffroom.

Sophie made herself some extra-strong coffee. This was surreal. And when she next saw Charlie Radley, he had some explaining to do.

Not that Sophie had the chance to discuss it with Charlie the next time she saw him. It was Saturday night and they were both on a late.

He rapped on her office door and when she called, 'Come in,' he opened the door and put his head round it. 'Sophie? I know you've got a ward round due, but I need your help.'

'What?'

'There aren't any female doctors in ED tonight. And I've got a case where I definitely need a female doctor with me.' He bit his lip. 'I'm sorry to ask you. It's not going to be pleasant.'

Sophie's stomach lurched. She knew what he was going to say. 'It's a…' She couldn't push the word out. Not that word. 'An assault.' A sexual one.

He nodded bleakly. 'Come with me to ED?'

'We're surgeons.' Sophie gulped. 'You're a *plastic* surgeon. Does that mean…?'

'He had a knife.' Charlie nodded. 'I'm afraid so. But ED tells me the cuts are to her face and neck.'

At least a knife hadn't been involved when she—

Now was *not* the time to remember that. She pulled herself together. They had a patient downstairs who needed a lot of understanding and help. 'Is the police surgeon down there?'

'The only one they have is male. And the gynae lot are all male tonight, too. So we need a female chaperone. Unless…?'

She nodded. 'I'll do the examination and take the samples. If she wants me to.'

Charlie took her hand for a second and squeezed it. 'Thanks. I know it's asking a lot.'

Yeah. But you don't know just *how* much you're asking, Sophie thought. She'd dealt with assault cases since specialising in surgery, but she hadn't dealt with a rape. She hadn't had to face this.

She had a choice. She could walk away. But that would mean leaving the victim with no choice—and Sophie thought the woman had already been through enough. Why make it worse for her? Sophie was a professional. A doctor. She'd done some work with police surgeons, and knew how the system worked.

Learn to take the emotion out of it.

Charlie's words echoed in her mind.

He was right. And she'd blocked it for years. She could block it again tonight. She could do this.

The young woman in the private ED room was still shaking when Sophie and Charlie walked in. Her face and throat were covered in blood from knife cuts, her clothes were ripped and Sophie could see grazes over the girl's skin.

'I'm Charlie Radley, plastic surgeon, and this is my colleague, Sophie Harrison. Would it be all right if Sophie examines you?'

'I just want to wash myself clean.' The woman's voice trembled.

'Of course you do. What's your name?' Charlie asked gently.

'Lois.'

'Lois, it's your choice. You don't have to be examined. But if you do let us examine you and take some samples, it can help stop this happening to someone else. No woman should ever have to go through this.'

'He cut me.' The words were barely a whisper.

'And I can help you, make sure the scars are as minimal as possible,' Charlie said quietly.

'He—he kicked me. Here.' She put a shaking hand out towards her back.

'That's why I'd like to examine you,' Sophie said. 'To make sure you don't have any internal injuries.'

A tear trickled down Lois's face. 'I didn't do anything wrong. I was only dancing. With my mates. And he—he…'

'It's OK. You're being very brave,' Sophie said. 'I know it's hard.' God, she knew how hard it was to say what someone had tried to do to you. Not knowing if they were going to believe you, blame you, say it was your fault. Hoping they'd understand. But then you looked up and saw the disgust and loathing in their eyes…

She took Lois's hand. 'But it's important that we stop him. That he doesn't get the chance to do this to anyone else.'

'It wasn't my fault.'

'I know. And we're going to help you, Lois, if you'll let us,' she said gently. 'I know the only thing you want to do right now is scrub all the traces of him off you. I promise you can do that. But if you let me take samples first, we've got a better chance of stopping him. Nobody's going to push you into doing anything you don't want. But if you let me take the samples, you're leaving all your choices open. Don't let him take your choices away, too.'

Eventually, Lois gave her written consent and allowed them to go through the procedure. She stepped onto brown paper behind a screen, removed her clothes and put them on the paper, then put a gown on and allowed Sophie to examine her. Sophie's documentation was meticulous; the policewoman took down the statements and photographed the knife injuries. As Charlie had said, they were to the face and upper body. There was also bruising on Lois's back, and Sophie noted the possibility of renal injury. She wouldn't know for sure without intravenous urography and urine tests to check for haematuria, or the presence of blood in the urine.

Gently, Sophie took vaginal and oral swabs, and asked Lois for a urine specimen so she could do a pregnancy test as well as check for the presence of blood in her urine—just in case Lois had been pregnant without knowing it before the attack. Then she cleaned up Lois's face and neck.

'I'm going to clean your wounds a little more thoroughly,' Charlie said. 'Not that Sophie hasn't done a good job, but if there's the slightest bit of dirt in the wounds you'll end up with tattooing on your skin. I'm afraid it doesn't look very nice— and you might worry that I'm going to make everything much worse, using a wire scrubber to clean your face—but I promise you this is the best thing to do. Then I'll stitch the cuts,'

Charlie said. 'The edges are straight, not irregular, so the scarring won't be as bad as you think. Early on, the scars will look red and they'll be hard around the edges, but they'll soften and fade over time, so eventually they'll be paler than your surrounding skin. In a year we'll have a better idea about whether we need to do more surgery to improve their appearance or whether I need to do something called dermabrasion—which means taking off the top layer of the skin.'

'A year?' Lois asked, sounding horrified.

'A year,' Charlie said quietly.

'You'll still be beautiful,' Sophie promised, still holding Lois's hand. 'Charlie's stitching is amazing. He's the best plastic surgeon I've ever worked with.' And it wasn't just an empty reassurance: she'd seen the way Charlie worked. 'I trust him.'

'I'll put a dressing on when I've finished—it's what we call tulle gras. It's a light dressing of a fabric called tulle. It has petroleum jelly in it, so it lets any fluids pass through to the outside, but doesn't let anything back in. And, more importantly, it doesn't stick to the skin. I should be able to take the stitches out in two or three days,' Charlie said, 'and then you'll need micropore tape on the scars for a few days to help protect and support the wounds.'

'Is it going to hurt?' Lois asked.

'I'll try very hard not to hurt you,' Charlie promised.

Sophie stayed with Lois while Charlie cleaned and stitched the wounds and Lois gave her statement to the police. When the urine tests came back, Sophie was relieved to see that there wasn't any evidence of blood in it. 'I think you're going to be lucky with just bruising,' she said, 'but I'd like to keep you in overnight, just in case you start to get any pain in your back around your kidneys.' Sometimes, with trauma to the kidneys, haematuria was delayed. 'If you'd like to come up to the ward with us, I'll admit you. You'll be safe there,' she added. 'Nobody can hurt you. Do you want me to call anyone for you?'

Lois shook her head.

'What about your mum?'

Not that Sophie had called *her* mum. She hadn't breathed a word about it. She'd felt too ashamed. Dirty.

'I can't. I can't ring her. Her boyfriend…' Lois shuddered.

Obviously a strained relationship that wouldn't take the extra weight of what had just happened to Lois, Sophie thought. 'It's OK. Everything's going to be all right,' Sophie said. 'I know right now it feels like the end of the world but, I promise you, you'll get through this.'

Not meeting Charlie's gaze, she helped Lois up, and together they walked up to the surgical ward.

CHAPTER EIGHT

'SOPHIE?' Charlie stood in her office doorway.

She looked up from her paperwork. 'What?'

'Are you OK?'

'Why wouldn't I be?'

He didn't know. But he had a strong feeling that something was wrong. Very wrong. He closed the door behind him. 'May I sit down?'

She shrugged. 'If you want.'

She sounded so brittle, as if she'd crack at the slightest pressure. He needed to be careful here. 'I could be barking up the wrong tree, so if I am just tell me to go away. But I think Lois is a heartstrings case for you.' Like that burns case had been for him.

Sophie refused to look at him. 'It shouldn't happen to any woman.'

'I agree with you. But I think there's more to it than that.'

'Don't be ridiculous.'

'Sophie, you should have gone off duty an hour ago. But you sat with Lois from the moment you finished your ward round until she fell asleep.'

'As I would do with any patient in that position. She didn't have anyone with her.'

Her jaw was set, so clearly she didn't want to talk about it. But Charlie couldn't leave it. She was hurt. And he wanted to make her feel better—the same way she'd made him feel better the other night. 'You're off duty as of now. So am I. I'm getting a taxi back to my place, and you're coming with me.'

'What?' Her eyes narrowed.

'I owe you,' he said simply. 'You fed me and gave me some space when I had the day from hell. I'm doing the same for you. And we're friends—aren't we?'

She lifted her chin. 'What, after you set your sister on me?'

He frowned. 'I beg your pardon?'

'The other day. When you were at Harley Street.'

It was his turn to narrow his eyes. 'How do you know where I was?'

'Vicky told me how you spend your days off.'

He waited a beat. 'And you're going to lecture me about private medicine now?'

'I would have done,' she admitted. 'Until Vicky told me the rest of it. That you blagged private theatre time and didn't charge your patients. You specialise in kids.'

Charlie exhaled sharply. His *interfering* baby sister! 'She had no business telling you about that.'

'Why was she checking me out?'

Charlie closed his eyes. Oh, great. Sophie was bright enough to see through whatever pathetic excuse Vicky had used. Of course she'd guessed what Vicky was really up to. Seb had obviously spilled the beans to Vicky, who'd decided to give Sophie the once-over and make sure that she wasn't another Julia, someone who would hurt him desperately. 'Don't get the wrong idea. My siblings are a bit over-protective.'

'Making sure you don't hook up with a gold-digger?'

Sick joke. He may have a title and a country estate with a

vast pile of a building in the middle, but as for the actual fold-ing stuff…no chance. Not after the inheritance tax they'd had to pay on the estate. And the house just *ate* money. Yes, he was wealthy on paper—but *only* on paper. His money was tied up in the estate. Anyway, he knew Sophie wasn't a gold-dig-ger. 'No. I'll scalp Seb later. And I apologise if my sister grilled you.'

'What did you tell them about me?'

'I didn't tell Vicky anything. And Seb just…' Charlie rubbed a hand over his eyes. 'I don't want to have this con-versation, Sophie. Right now, I just want to feed you and make you feel better.'

'Like I did to you?'

'Yeah. No strings. I'm not going to leap on you or anything. I'll just give you some space to be you.' He wrinkled his nose. 'I can't offer you any decent cake, I'm afraid. But, unless Vicky raided my stash, I have chocolate.'

'You live with your brother and sister?'

He shook his head. 'I live on my own. Not even a hamster to keep me company—it wouldn't be fair to have a pet, work-ing doctor's hours.' Though how he missed having a dog. 'Come on. Turn off the computer and come home with me. I make a mean bacon sandwich. And I'm willing to bet it's bet-ter than whatever you'd get in the hospital canteen or the greasy spoon down the road.'

For a moment he thought she was going to refuse. Then she leaned back against her chair, almost in defeat. 'OK. Thank you.'

The taxi was waiting for them outside the side entrance to the hospital. Charlie held the door open for Sophie, then slid in beside her. He gave his address to the taxi driver, then lapsed into silence. He wasn't going to pressure her to talk now. But she'd definitely talk in his kitchen. The bacon sandwich would make sure of that.

Sophie's eyes widened as she realised where Charlie lived—a very fashionable part of Hampstead, where the house prices were astronomical—but she made no comment as he showed her up to his second-floor flat.

It wasn't furnished the way she'd expected, though. Not dark colours and full of antiques and heirlooms. The walls were painted a sunny primrose yellow, the carpet was plain Berber wool and the furniture was modern. Not expensive-looking either. There were a couple of watercolours on the walls which she assumed were originals, but they were rural waterscapes and easy on the eye. About the only concessions to family were three framed photographs: one of Charlie with Vicky; one of Charlie with a slightly younger man who looked so like him Sophie assumed it must be Seb; and one of what looked like Charlie as a teenager, with an older man she assumed was his father.

Not that she had a chance to see much as he shepherded her into his kitchen. This room was equally unassuming, though there was a scrubbed pine table in the middle and he had one of those huge American fridges her mum drooled over but hadn't bought because they were too big to fit in her kitchen.

'Are you on call?' he asked.

'Not officially. But I've asked the night staff to bleep me if Lois's obs take a dip. Any sign of haematuria and I'll be there.'

'OK. We'll skip the wine, then. Tea or coffee?'

'Whatever's to hand.'

'Coffee's safer.' He smiled. 'Seb says my tea is undrinkable.'

She knew he was trying to make her feel relaxed. But how

could she? How could she chill out when tonight had brought it all back to her?

He made them both a mug of coffee—fresh rather than instant, she noticed, and the bag of beans he took from the fridge and ground by hand looked as if it had come from a specialist shop. But what else should she expect from a baron? He probably did his grocery shopping at Fortnum and Mason or Harrods.

But, oh, the coffee smelt good. And it tasted even better.

'My local butcher does the best bacon in the world,' Charlie announced, as if reading her mind. He placed the bacon under the grill. 'I try to buy from the local shops where I can, rather than the supermarkets.'

Because he believed in being part of the community? Yeah, she could believe that. Charlie Radley had integrity. And he was nothing like the person she'd thought he'd be.

She watched him as he sliced tomatoes, buttered granary bread and spread a layer of wild rocket on top. 'It has more taste than lettuce,' he said.

She really hadn't thought she could face eating anything tonight. But Charlie's sandwich smelled fantastic.

'It's all organic,' he said, layering the sandwich together then putting the plate in front of her. 'Promise. Just one bite, Sophie. That's all I'm asking.'

She took a bite of the sandwich. 'You're right. You make a mean bacon sarnie.' And, right now, it was just what she needed. 'Thanks.'

He smiled, but didn't push her. He just let her eat her sandwich and drink her coffee. When she'd finished, he topped up her mug and brought out a box of dark chocolate thins. Organic, seventy per cent cocoa solids—and the most incredible chocolate hit.

This was comfort food at its very best. And he was clearly hoping it would make her talk. Tell him what was wrong.

But how could she explain?

She was so near to telling him. But something was holding her back. Didn't she trust him? Was she worried about his reaction? 'It's better out than in,' Charlie said softly.

'I…' She shook her head.

'If it helps, I know the value of privacy. Whatever you tell me stays just between you and me.'

She gulped. 'It was a long time ago. I'm over it.'

'Even so. Right now, I think you need to talk. And I'm listening.' He wanted to pull her onto his lap and hold her close, but he knew it would set all her defences in motion. So he sat quietly and waited, his hands cupping the mug of coffee.

'I was a student,' she said eventually, her eyes glistening with unshed tears. 'My final year. I'd been working late in the library. I was walking back to my flat. I'd done it hundreds of times. There was nothing different about that night.' There was a far-away look on her face, mixed with disgust and horror. 'And then…there were three of them. They lived near me. Always out partying. The sort that used to be known as Hooray Henrys. There was a gang of them—some were medics, some were lawyers. The medics gave me a hard time in class because I was common and they weren't.' She grimaced. 'It didn't go down well that I got better marks than they did in exams. Though God only knows how they scraped through—I often wonder if Daddy greased a few palms.'

Charlie felt all his muscles tense. Suddenly he knew what she was going to tell him. And he wanted to punch something. Someone. Preferably whoever had hurt her.

But that wouldn't solve anything now. She'd started to open up, and he wasn't going to interrupt her.

'That night…they'd been out drinking. There were just three of them, staggering down the road. Egging each other on. I should've just ignored them when they started cat-calling me. If I hadn't responded, they'd have got bored. They'd have just drunk themselves into a stupor. But, no, I had to make some stupid, smart-alec comment. The next thing I knew…' Her voice was shaking. 'I was on the ground. They were on me. All three of them. Saying I was a tease, that I wore tight jeans to class just to turn them on. And teases get what they ask for. They knew I wanted it. So I was going to get it. They were going to take what they wanted.' She wrapped her arms around herself. 'They ripped my clothes. They touched me. I tried to fight them off, but they were too strong. Three against one. They—they told me they were going to have me. All at the same time. They were going to—going to… Oh, dear God.' She choked. 'I don't know why they stopped. I think they must have heard somebody coming. But they got off me. I left my books where they'd fallen and just ran while I had the chance. I don't know if they followed me. I just concentrated on getting home. I locked my door and I scrubbed myself until my skin bled, and still I couldn't get clean. And I couldn't stop hearing them.' Her voice dropped to a whisper. 'Them and their posh voices.'

No wonder she hated upper-class men. Charlie couldn't handle the distance between them any more. He scraped his chair backwards, walked round to her and put his arms round her, holding her close. 'Oh, Sophie. That kind of behaviour is unacceptable from *any* man.'

'They were rich and they were posh, so they thought they had the right to do anything they liked to me.'

'Well, they thought wrong. Very wrong. Nobody has that sort of right.' He stroked her hair. 'Did you report it?'

'They didn't actually r—' She swallowed the word back. 'There was no p-penetration involved. Technically, there was no crime.'

'Technically, it was still assault,' Charlie said. 'They touched you without your consent. So you could have reported it, sweetheart.'

'I tried. I talked to my tutor about it. But who are you going to believe?' Her eyes were bleak. 'Three blokes whose fathers donate a lot of money to the university, or one common East End girl?' She shuddered. 'He called them in to explain themselves. They said…' She took a shaky breath. 'They said I'd been out drinking with them. That I'd been leading them on. It was a game that got out of hand. They were having a bit of fun, that was all, and I was telling tales because I hadn't got what I wanted. They *lied*. And…and the tutor believed them.'

'That's outrageous.' Charlie lifted her from her chair and sat down, pulling her onto his lap. He held her close to him, his cheek against her hair. 'It should never have happened.'

'What could I do about it? I didn't want to be thrown out of med school.'

He frowned. 'Why would they do that when *you* were the victim?'

'Because I was making a fuss. Being a troublemaker.'

'No, you were telling the truth.' He stroked her hair. 'What they did—what your tutor did—was morally wrong. Did you tell your parents?'

Sophie shook her head. 'I didn't want them to worry. I was up in Manchester—they'd have wanted me to come back home and forget the exams. And then my studying would all have been for nothing. All the sacrifices they made so I could go to med school, they'd have been for nothing. I couldn't do that to them.'

'What about the men? They hurt you and got away with it. They could have done it to someone else.'

'But they didn't.' Sophie shook her head. 'I think it was a wake-up call, because they didn't think I'd actually tell someone about them. Yeah, they got away with it—but it made them think twice. They kept a low profile after that and so did I.' She shivered and nestled closer to him. 'I learned self-defence after that. I swore nobody would ever treat me like that again.'

'Tell me their names,' Charlie said softly, between clenched teeth, 'and I'll find them. And forget the Hippocratic oath—I'll do some surgery on them. With a rusty scalpel and no anaesthetic.'

'It wouldn't change what happened.'

'No. But it'd make me feel better. I'm sorry, Sophie. I'm sorry they did that to you. I'm sorry they hurt you. And if I could make it better, I would.' He rubbed his cheek against hers. 'But I don't know how to make you feel better.'

'Just…keep holding me.' The words sounded almost like tissue paper ripping. As if she didn't want to say them, but couldn't help herself.

She wanted him to hold her.

'I'll never hurt you, Sophie,' he whispered, brushing his lips against her cheek. 'Not all men are like that.'

'I know.'

Mmm, but he had the feeling she didn't include men from his social background in that statement. 'Not all upper-class men are like that,' he added. Though, he thought with a stab of guilt, his brother was a louse towards women. 'Did you get any counselling?'

'How could I? Nobody believed me.'

'Not even your boyfriend? Your best friend?'

'I felt too dirty to tell them.' Sophie swallowed hard. 'I…I dumped my boyfriend after that. I couldn't stand him touching me.'

'And you haven't told a boyfriend since?'

'What do you think?'

No. Because it would be very, very difficult to talk about it. But she'd told *him* about it. She'd trusted him enough.

'*I* believe you,' he said softly.

She made no comment, simply put her arms round him and cuddled into him. 'I worked hard. I wanted to make sure they couldn't spoil my career as well as everything else. I wasn't going to let them make me fail my exams.'

'And you've done well. More than well. You're an excellent surgeon.' He brushed his lips against her cheek again. 'If I hadn't come along, you'd be consultant now.'

'I'm not holding that against you.' Her voice was shaky, but there was an edge of laughter in it.

'Good.' He rubbed the tip of his nose against hers. 'You're a brave woman, Sophie Harrison.'

'I didn't feel it tonight. When I saw Lois… It's the first time I've had to face anything like this. I know the drill, but when I did my ED rotation I was lucky: I didn't get any cases like this. Fights, yes. But not a r—' She dragged in a breath, as if unwilling to say the word. 'I thought I was over it all. It was so long ago now.'

'Doesn't matter. Something like this will always bring it back.' He stroked her hair. 'I hate telling children that their father didn't wake up from the operation.'

She made the connection instantly. 'You lost your dad?'

Charlie nodded. 'We were out on the estate. Not doing anything special, just walking. He collapsed and I didn't know what to do. I didn't have a clue about first aid. The last time I'd done anything was in the Cub Scouts for my first-aid badge, and I couldn't even remember how to put my father in the recovery position. I ran to the house and called an ambulance—we didn't have mobile phones back then—but he died about five minutes after I got back to his side. He was dead before the ambulance even got there.' He drew in a deep breath. 'They said it was a massive heart attack. There was nothing anyone could have done to save him.'

'How old were you?' Sophie asked.

'Sixteen. It was the summer after I'd taken my O-levels. I was going be a lawyer—but it made me think about what I was doing. What I really wanted to do. And I wanted to stop someone else going through what my family went through that summer. I decided to be a doctor. So I rang my school and changed my A-level courses.' He smiled grimly. 'My mother wasn't pleased, because I was supposed to join the family firm. We had row after row about it. Especially when I told her I wasn't planning to practise in Harley Street, that I was going to work in the National Health Service. But Seb and Vicky backed me up. They wanted to be doctors, too.'

'Following in your footsteps?'

He shook his head. 'Vicky always wanted to be a doctor, right from when she was small. When our mother made her go to ballet lessons, Vicky took a pair of scissors to her tutu and ballet shoes. She threatened to cut all her hair off if anyone made her go back again.' He smiled at the memory of a very determined five-year-old. 'Though Mother didn't learn and tried to send her to a finishing school instead of letting her do the A-levels she wanted. Vicky got herself expelled in the first week, came home and talked the local college into letting her start the A-level courses late. She got the best grades in the country and an unconditional offer to study medicine in London. Seb…' His smile faded. 'Well, Seb's just a law unto himself. I love him dearly, but there are times when I could murder him.'

'He's that difficult?'

'Trust me, you don't want to know,' Charlie said feelingly.

'Why did you choose plastic surgery?' Sophie asked.

'I was going to be a cardiologist,' Charlie said. 'Like my father. But I did a surgical rotation and I discovered how much I liked surgery. Plastics is even better—because you make a real difference to people's lives. They've been hurt, but you can patch them up, make them look good as new. Make their body work the way it used to before the accident.' He paused. 'What about you? Why surgery?'

'I used to do a lot of jigsaws when I was a kid. I liked putting things together and fixing them.' Sophie shrugged. 'I wanted to fix people, too. Mum suggested becoming a nurse, but I knew early on I wanted to be a surgeon. I like general surgery. You get to do a bit of everything.'

'Yeah.' He stroked her hair again. 'I'm sorry you had to go through this tonight.'

'I had to face it some time.'

'But I'm glad I was there, too,' he said softly.

She simply looked at him, those beautiful brown eyes filling with tears. 'Me, too,' she said hoarsely.

One tear spilled down her cheek, and he wiped it away with the pad of his thumb. And then, unable to help himself, he kissed away the smear of moisture. Just a gentle brush of his lips—but, Lord, her skin was soft. So sweet and soft. And he wanted more.

He kissed the tip of her nose. Just once.

And then she tipped her head back slightly. Offering her mouth.

Hell, hell, hell. She'd just told him about how her fellow students had forced themselves on her, nearly raped her. Something she'd told almost nobody else, from the sound of things. She was *crying*, for God's sake. And what was he doing? Coming on to her. Kissing her.

He was disgusted with himself. He should be comforting her, not trying to seduce her.

'I'm sorry,' he whispered against her cheek, holding her close. 'I'm so sorry.'

And then her lips were against his ear. 'I'm not. Make me forget them, Charlie. Make me forget tonight.'

Was she asking him to…?

And then her mouth found his, and the blood drained straight out of his head.

CHAPTER NINE

THIS was all wrong—they really weren't supposed to be doing this. And then Charlie stopped thinking as Sophie's fingers caressed the back of his neck. She nibbled at his lower lip, and he opened his mouth with a sigh, letting her deepen the kiss.

He needed this. He really *needed* this. And so, he thought, did she. To hell with the real world. Right here, right now, it was just the two of them. And they'd make each other forget all their worries.

He took the clip from her hair and dropped it on the table, then loosened her hair so it fell over her shoulders. 'I could play with your hair all night,' he murmured. 'It's so soft.' He couldn't resist wrapping it round his hands. Though what he really wanted was to see her hair spread over his pillow, framing her in gold as he eased into her.

She undid his tie; he let her pull the silk from his collar and drop it on the table. Then his heart went into overdrive as she undid the top button of his shirt—and continued working her way downwards.

'I wondered,' she said, tugging the soft cotton from the waistband of his dark suit trousers.

'What?' He rubbed the tip of his nose against hers.

'If you worked out. But this is proper muscle, not gym-gorilla stuff.'

He smiled. So she'd been imagining him in the gym, had she? 'I don't lift weights, but I run most days,' he said. 'On a treadmill.' So he could get his endorphin fix in peace, not harassed by the paparazzi wanting a snap of the baron looking all hot and bothered.

Though right now he was definitely hot and bothered. For a very different reason.

She ran her fingers over his pecs, smoothing over the light sprinkling of dark hair. 'Mmm.'

He ran the tip of his tongue over his lower lip. 'Hey. What's sauce for the goose…'

She tilted her head back and gave him the wickedest look he'd ever seen. 'Yes?'

'My turn. I'd like to see you, Sophie,' he said huskily. 'Touch you. May I?'

She held his gaze for a long, long moment. He could see desire blurring with fear, and gently stroked her cheek. 'Sophie. I promise I won't hurt you. I won't do anything you don't want me to do. I'll stop if you ask me to. And I always keep my word.'

He kept himself in check, although his whole body was almost humming with a desperate need to touch her. No way would he do anything without her explicit permission.

Finally, she nodded—such a tiny movement he could barely see it. 'Yes.' Her voice rasped. Why? Because she was scared? Because she wanted him? A mixture of the two?

I'm going to make this good for you, he promised her silently. I'm going to make you forget the memories that hurt you so much again tonight.

Slowly, carefully, he undid the top button of her shirt. Brushed her skin with the backs of his fingers. 'So soft,' he said. 'Like velvet.' He traced the curve of her collarbones, then slowly undid another button. And another.

When her shirt was completely open, he sucked in his breath, 'God, you're beautiful, Sophie. And I want you. Very, very much.' He traced a necklace of kisses around her throat and she slid her fingers back into his hair, urging him on. He licked the sensitive spot at the side of her neck and felt her shiver in his arms.

And he wanted more.

He stood up, lifting her as he did so. 'Sophie. Forgive me. I want to do the macho thing and carry you to my bed.'

'Sounds good to me,' she said huskily, and leaned down to kiss him.

He had no memory of leaving the kitchen or carrying her to his bedroom. Time just seemed to stop as she kissed him. But then they were outside his bedroom door. He kicked it open and carried her over to the bed.

The curtains were open, but he couldn't bear to let her go for long enough to go over to the window and close them. So he carried her over, still kissing her. Dragged the curtains shut. And gently put her down where he wanted her: right in the middle of his king-size bed.

His bed was huge, Sophie thought as Charlie reached over and switched on the lamp. An enormous *bateau-lit,* made from polished cherrywood, it dominated the room. The rest of the furniture was painted cream, the walls were pale aqua and there were more waterscapes on the walls. It was peaceful. A restful room. The kind of room where you could lounge on a Sunday morning with the newspaper, leaning back against thick feather pillows and just chilling out with a cup of coffee and a shared plate of flaky, buttery croissants.

There was a small sound system on the table next to the bed—she'd bet anything that he listened to really highbrow classical music. Opera. Not her type of thing at all. In fact, nothing in this room had a place in her life.

She should feel like a fish out of water.

But all she could feel, right now, was need. A desperate need for Charlie. A need for him to cover her body with his, make love with her, fill her, push all the shadows out of her body and out of her head. She knelt and slid her arms around his neck, then brushed her mouth against his, nibbling at his lower lip until he kissed her back.

Slowly, she slid the open shirt from his shoulders and dropped it on the carpet. Charlie had an amazing body, she thought. Lean and muscular, with broad shoulders tapering to a narrow waist. There was a sprinkling of hair on his chest that arrowed down over his torso, disappearing beneath the waistband of his dark trousers. Just enough to be sexy. Tempting. Delineating his musculature.

'My turn,' he whispered softly.

'Yes,' she hissed as he slid her own shirt from her shoulders and dropped it on top of his. She closed her eyes and tipped her head back. Charlie kissed her throat, nuzzling his way down to the valley between her breasts.

'Touch me, Charlie. Make love with me,' she whispered.

He unclasped her bra but she didn't notice or care where it went—not when his hands were cupping her breasts. It felt so good to have his hands on her like this. Skin to skin. No barriers.

He dipped his head, taking one hard nipple into his mouth.

Her breath shuddered as his tongue circled her areola and skated over the tip of her breast. He blew gently on her wet skin, driving her to the point where she was almost hyperventilating, then did the same to the other breast.

'Don't tease,' she begged.

'Don't tease?' He rocked back onto his haunches and grinned at her. 'Says the woman who smells of chocolate,' he said. 'Vanilla and chocolate. Do you have any idea how much you blow my mind?'

If it was anything like what he'd just done to hers—then, yes. 'Charlie.' She ran her fingernails lightly down his back. 'I want you.'

His pupils were so huge that his eyes looked almost black, instead of the deep cornflower blue she always noticed in Theatre. 'Believe me, honey, it's mutual.' His voice was deep, husky with desire. And it sent a thrill through her that she could make him feel like this—Charlie, who was always so self-contained on the wards. So professional. Smooth, urbane, cultured… Right now, he was nothing like that. He was in control of himself, but only just. She could tell by the colour slashing across his cheekbones that desire was raging as fiercely within him as it was within her.

And it was all for her.

With shaking hands, she undid the button of his trousers. Lowered the zip. Slid the fabric downwards so it pooled around his knees.

He did the same to her skirt.

She stroked the curve of his buttocks. 'That's one hell of a gluteus maximus you have there, Mr Radley,' she murmured.

'Funny you should say that,' he retorted, returning the favour. 'I was thinking exactly the same about you, Dr Harrison.'

'Were you, now?' She hooked her thumbs into the waistband of his boxer shorts and drew them down, keeping her gaze fixed on his.

'Sophie. You do know you're driving me out of my mind, don't you?' he whispered.

And then he copied her action, sliding her tights and knickers down to her knees in one smooth movement.

'We have a bit of a problem,' Sophie said, while she could still frame the words. 'We choreographed this badly.' No way could she move, with her clothes wrapped round her knees. And the same was true for him.

'I never said I was perfect.' He kissed the tip of her nose. 'And, yes, you're right. We have a bit of a problem. Close your eyes and trust me.'

'What?'

'Close your eyes and trust me,' he repeated, 'because there's only one place we can go from here.'

She closed her eyes. And felt herself falling, falling sideways—straight into the softest, deepest, plushest pillow she'd ever come across.

She opened her eyes. 'Charlie!'

He grinned at her, his face level with her own. 'We were stuck. It was the only way out, pulling you down here with me.' He stretched out and shucked his remaining clothes in one smooth movement. 'Better,' he said. 'But this is going to be better still.' He shimmied his way down the bed, lifted her legs, and stripped her skirt, tights and knickers from her.

She was about to make a smart remark about him seeming rather practised when she felt the touch of his mouth at the back of her knee and all the clever words went straight out of her head.

Oh-h-h.

Since when had *that* been an erotic spot?

His fingers cruised up the inside of her thigh, and she stopped thinking altogether. Her hands fisted into the pillows as he stroked her skin; she closed her eyes and shifted onto her back, begging him with her body to go further. Touch her. Taste her. Take her to paradise and back.

'Sophie.' He shifted to lie beside her again, on his side, and tilted her hips so that she was facing him again. Then he slid a hand between her thighs to cup her sex, and she felt a pulse start to beat very hard against him. 'Sophie,' he whispered. 'I want to touch you.'

'Oh. Yes. Please,' she said, unable to get the sentence out in one piece.

'Mmm.' He brushed his mouth against hers. Her breath hissed out of her as he drew one finger along her cleft. So near. Not enough.

'I want to touch you. Taste you. Make love with you.' He rubbed his face against her hair. 'I love your hair. It drives me crazy when I see it pinned back at work. I want to see you how you were the other night. All mussed and rumpled and wide-eyed.' He nibbled her earlobe. 'And I want you to rumple me, too.'

Oh, yes. There was going to be some serious rumpling going on tonight. She couldn't remember when she'd ever felt this turned on. She could feel every pulse in her body thrumming, wanting him. Yearning for him.

'I want you,' she whispered. 'I need you inside me.'

He pushed one finger in. 'Like this?'

She gasped. 'Not enough.'

He kissed her hard. 'Give me a second.' She heard a rattle and a muffled curse, and opened her eyes. He was rummaging in a drawer. Panic was beginning to spread over his face as he clearly couldn't find what he was looking for.

Then his expression cleared. 'For a moment, there…' He blew out a breath, and ripped the foil packet open. 'If I hadn't had anything to protect you—if we'd had to stop—I think I would have spontaneously combusted.'

'Me, too,' Sophie said. And then shocked herself with the realisation that if he hadn't had a condom, she would've broken all her personal rules right there and then, and told him not to stop.

He kissed her again. 'You're sure about this?'

'I'm sure.'

'You're shaking.'

'What were you saying about spontaneous combustion?'

He gave her a slow, lazy grin. 'Let's make a fire, Sophie.'

Yes. She wanted this. She wanted *him*. She closed her eyes and tipped her head back, inviting another kiss. Let him turn her onto her back.

And then, when he positioned himself between her thighs, she opened her eyes. Saw him looming over her. And the moment shattered like crystal. It wasn't Charlie in her mind's eye. It was someone else. Pinning her down, ripping at her clothes —

'No!'

Charlie heard the yelp of panic in Sophie's voice, and stopped.

'Sophie?'

Her eyes were open, but unfocused. Her face was ashen and she was twisting her head from side to side. 'No!'

'OK. It's OK.' He shifted so that he was sitting beside her, pulled her onto his lap and wrapped the duvet round them both. 'Hey. It's OK.'

'I can't do this,' she said. Her breathing was more like sobbing between the words.

'It's OK,' he repeated.

She shook her head. 'I thought I could but… Oh, God. I can't. I *can't.*'

She was shivering, on the verge of tears.

And Charlie was torn between wanting to hold her and wanting to rip three certain ex-medical students to shreds. His fists balled, and he forced himself to relax them and breathe normally. She'd been through enough. He wasn't going to make it worse for her by playing the tough guy.

'Shh. You're safe. You're with me,' he soothed, and cradled her until her shudders had died down.

'I'm sorry. I…' Her bottom lip quivered.

'No need to apologise.' He stroked her hair. 'We went too far, too fast, that's all. I'm not going to do anything you don't want me to do. I promise.'

'I'm sorry,' she said again, her voice miserable.

'Nothing to be sorry about.'

'I'll, um, get dressed.'

She wouldn't look at him, he noticed. Embarrassed? Ashamed? He wasn't sure. But she had no need to be either. He kissed the top of her head. 'I've got a better idea.'

'What?' Her muscles were tense and her voice was suspicious.

'Stay with me tonight.'

'What?'

'Stay with me tonight,' he repeated. 'We're not going to have sex. We're just going to sleep in each other's arms.'

'But…' She met his gaze.

He could have wept. Did she *really* think he'd chuck her out of his bed because she wasn't going to have sex with him? Was her opinion of him really that low?

'Listen, when I brought you here tonight, there were no strings. I didn't expect you to have sex with me, just because

I made you a sandwich. You were upset and I wanted to do what you did for me the other night. I wanted to make you feel better, give you some space.' He stroked her upper arms. 'We're both drained. We've told each other things that maybe we haven't said to anyone else. Yes, I wanted to make love with you. I think you wanted it, too. It hasn't worked out that way, but we'll deal with it. Right now, I could do with some comfort—and I think you could, too.'

'I… Yes,' she admitted, and leaned back against him.

'So let's heal each other. Just sleep. Nothing more than that.' He kissed the top of her head. 'And we'll see where things take us in the future. Slowly.'

Sophie really hadn't expected Charlie to be so nice about it. She'd led him on—she'd even begged him to make love with her. She'd told him she wanted him inside her.

And then the nightmare had returned. She'd panicked. Backed off.

Shouldn't he be furious with her for calling it off at the last minute?

But no. He was holding her, understanding in his voice and his eyes. And he wanted her to sleep with him, just sleep. Give each other comfort.

Even though she tried to force them back, tears welled in her eyes and splashed down onto her skin. They must have fallen onto him, too, because he held her close, soothing her. 'Don't cry, Sophie. You're safe, here with me. Nothing and nobody's going to hurt you.' He shifted so that they were lying flat, his body curled spoonlike into hers, his arm placed protectively round her ribcage and pulling her back against him. 'We've both had a rough week. Let's just go to sleep. It'll be better in the morning.'

Would it? She wasn't so sure.

'Do you want to keep the light on?'

'I… No.' She wanted the dark to cover her shame.

'The lamp's on your side.' He kissed her shoulder. 'Touch it three times.'

'Three times?'

'Mmm-hmm. There are three levels of brightness. At the moment it's on the lowest setting. You need to run through the other two and then it'll go off.'

She did as he instructed, and the room was bathed in blessed dark. 'That's clever.'

'Mmm. Though it doesn't work if you touch it with a book. And the brightness doesn't change if you hold your hand still.'

Despite her misery, she smiled. She could imagine Charlie wanting to know precisely what made it work. The surgeon in him needed to know exactly how things were put together. 'So how does it work, then?'

'Capacitance.' She could hear amusement in his voice. 'My baby sister explained it to me. Apparently, the neurons in your body complete the electrical circuit.'

'I see. It's still clever.'

A shudder ran through her, and he held her closer. 'Go to sleep,' he said softly.

Right now, she didn't think she'd ever be able to sleep. All her energies were focused on stopping herself crying, holding back the racking sobs that threatened to overwhelm her. But she squeezed her eyelids closed and concentrated on breathing rhythmically. The warmth of Charlie's body and the softness of his bed did the rest, and she slid into oblivion.

CHAPTER TEN

SOPHIE woke with a blinding headache. Someone was drilling, loudly, from the inside of her head. She kept her eyes shut, raked a hand into her hair and massaged her scalp with her fingertips. She knew from experience that if she increased the blood flow to her scalp, the pain would go away.

And all because she'd tried so hard not to cry last night. She'd lain in Charlie's arms and willed herself not to cry any more. And she hadn't. But the result was one hell of a tension headache.

Oh, God. *Charlie.*

The more she thought about last night, the more she wanted to bury her head under the duvet and never come out again. The whole thing had been a disaster from start to finish. One, she'd told him about what had happened when she'd been in med school. Two, she'd as good as told him that she hadn't slept with anyone since. OK, so she hadn't—but that had only been because she had been concentrating on her career, not her love life. It *wasn't* because she was scared of sex. Three, she'd begged him to make love with her. Four, she'd called it off at the very last second. Five, she'd cried all over him. And, if she thought about it, she could add a few more gaffes in there as well.

This had to rank as the most cringeworthy, hideously embarrassing situation in her entire life. How the hell was she going to be able to work with him now?

Worse still, how was she going to face him this morning?

He was still asleep. Heavily asleep, judging by his regular, even breathing. She hoped he wasn't one of those people who seemed fast asleep but woke at the slightest unfamiliar noise. Because she sure as hell wasn't going to face him stark naked. She'd get her clothes on, drag her dignity out of the rock it had crawled under and they'd discuss it like adults. Coolly, calmly and professionally.

Though there definitely wouldn't be any bacon sandwiches involved.

Cautiously, she slid out from under the duvet. Then she made her first mistake: she looked at Charlie. He was lying on his back, one arm thrown above his head and the other straight by his side. The duvet had slid halfway down his chest. His lips were very slightly parted, and he looked absolutely edible.

What she really wanted to do was lean over and kiss him awake.

If they'd made love last night, maybe she would have done.

But embarrassment at what had actually happened flooded through her again. She couldn't wake him. Not after last night's fiasco. She screwed her eyes tightly shut to focus herself, took a deep breath and then retrieved her clothes. Half of them were tangled with his. All of them were crumpled. So anybody who saw her would be in no doubt about what she'd done last night—why else would a woman walk through the streets on a Sunday morning wearing yesterday's crumpled clothes? She'd obviously spent the night at her lover's house and they'd got so carried away that she hadn't given her clothes a second thought.

Squirming inwardly, she tiptoed out of Charlie's bedroom and into the bathroom.

A shower was out of the question—it would be way too noisy. She didn't even dare risk splashing water on her face in case the sound woke him. Oh, what she would give for a pair of dark glasses to hide her eyes! She dressed swiftly. Her hair… Well, as long as she could find the clasp, she could pull it back so severely that nobody would notice just how mussed it was. All she had to do was brazen it out until she was back at her own flat. She could do that.

'You look a mess,' she whispered to her reflection. 'And the mess you're in is even worse. Why on earth did you go home with him at all last night? Why didn't you just say thank you for the sandwich and *leave*?'

She didn't want to answer those questions. Didn't want to face what she felt about Charlie Radley.

She stared at her reflection. If anything, she had less dignity when she was dressed than she had when she'd been naked. She didn't even know where to *begin* talking it over with Charlie. The longer she stayed in his flat, the more likely it was that he'd wake up. She wasn't ready to face him. And she didn't belong here. She didn't come from a world where the floors were proper polished hardwood, not laminate; where the rugs were expensive wool or silk, not some manmade fibre; and where the pictures on the wall were framed and signed originals rather than cheap and cheerful prints.

Last night had been one of her biggest mistakes ever.

And she needed some space between her and Charlie so she could work out how to deal with it.

Quietly, she left the bathroom. She knew she ought to leave him at least a note, but she really didn't know what to say to him. She'd call him later. Explain. For now, she just wanted to be home. Her *own* home. Where she belonged.

She walked through to the kitchen. No sign of her clip anywhere. She didn't want to risk searching for it either—the longer she stayed here, the more likely it was that he'd wake up and she'd have to face him. She needed to go. *Now.* She retrieved her shoes, handbag and jacket, and left Charlie's flat, clicking the door closed behind her.

Charlie stretched, yawned—and then sat bolt upright. He was alone in bed. Which meant something was very wrong—unless he'd only dreamed what had happened last night. Though he was pretty sure he hadn't been hallucinating, because he could still smell Sophie's scent. Vanilla and chocolate. There was a dent in the pillow next to his, where she'd slept. But her side of the bed was empty—and, judging from the coolness of the bed linen, had been empty for some time.

He frowned. He couldn't hear the boiler going, so she couldn't be in the bathroom. And there were no sounds from the kitchen, no scent of coffee. His frown deepened. Surely she was still here. They needed to talk after last night. They *definitely* needed to talk. No way would she have just left without a word. Not when she'd spent the night sleeping in his arms.

And she *had* slept with him. He'd lain awake until the small hours after she'd fallen asleep, with his body curled protectively around hers. The only thing was, when he had gone to sleep, he'd slept extremely deeply. Vicky and Seb were both convinced he could sleep through an earthquake. So maybe she'd got up, had a shower and was sitting in his living room, reading a journal and waiting for him to wake up—too shy or too embarrassed to wake him herself.

A swift glance round his bedroom told him that, whatever she was doing, she was fully dressed. Her clothes had gone, though his were still scattered on the floor where he'd dropped them last night.

Last night, when he'd had Sophie naked in his bed.

Frowning, he grabbed a clean pair of boxer shorts from his drawer, hauled them on and padded barefoot into his living room.

No sign of Sophie.

The bathroom was empty.

So was the kitchen.

Her shoes and her handbag were gone, too, which meant she'd left. Hurt prickled at the back of his neck. Why hadn't she waited for him? Unless she'd been on duty. Yeah, that must be it. She'd probably left him a note.

Nothing on the kitchen table.

Nothing on the worktops.

He returned to the living room. Nothing propped on the mantelpiece. No clearly visible scrap of paper or envelope or anything.

Maybe she'd left him a note on his pillow and it had fallen down the back of the mattress or something.

When a thorough search yielded nothing, he had to face it. Sophie had left. Without a word, without a note. She'd just left.

It took Charlie two cups of very strong coffee to get his head around it. Sophie was clearly embarrassed about what had happened between them—well, probably more about what *hadn't* happened—and this was a tactical retreat while she gathered her composure. If he called her, pushed her too hard, she'd probably back off even more. The best thing he could do was give her space. Let her come to terms with it. And—please, please, *please*—when she'd had time to think about it she'd realise that he wasn't angry with her and he wasn't going to push her into anything she wasn't comfortable with. And then, maybe, she'd trust him with herself.

He was just making his third cup of coffee when the phone rang.

He punched the air mentally and grabbed the receiver. *Yes. It was her.* 'Hello?'

'Good morning, bro',' Seb's voice drawled into his ear. 'You sounded rather eager just then. Expecting someone else to call, were you?'

'No,' Charlie lied, swallowing his disappointment. 'And to what do I owe the pleasure of hearing your dulcet tones at this time on a Sunday morning?'

'Thought I'd better warn you. Vic got a call from La Mama this morning. She's planning to come up to London some time soon.' There was a pause. 'Charlie, you're not going to subsidise her this time.'

'Mmm,' Charlie said.

'I mean it.' Seb made an exasperated noise. 'The woman's a vampire. She's bleeding your bank account dry.'

'She's our *mother*, Seb. I promised Dad I'd look after her.'

'There's looking after, and there's being taken advantage of. You're such a soft touch where women are concerned. You let them walk all over you.'

'I do not,' Charlie retorted, stung.

Though did Seb have a point? Was Charlie letting Sophie walk all over him?

'Yes, you do. And, before you say it, I *know* that woman is our mother. Sometimes it wouldn't hurt *her* to remember that and actually act like a mother instead of a sponge.'

'Seb, I'm not in the mood for this.'

There was a brief pause. 'Charlie? Are you all right?'

'Yes.'

'It doesn't sound like it.' Seb cleared his throat. 'Want to talk?'

To the world's biggest cynic? No way would Charlie ever discuss last night with Seb. Seb would just say he was being suckered. 'No. Last time I talked to you, you grassed to Vicky. Who decided to check Sophie out in person.'

'We did have your best interests at heart.' Seb paused. 'Is that what's wrong? Something's happened between you and Sophie?'

'No, it hasn't.' Which was most of the point. 'Will you get off my case?' Charlie snapped.

'Hey. If she's upset you, Vicky and I—'

'Will do absolutely nothing. Stay out of it, Sebastian,' Charlie warned. 'Everything's fine.' He just wished he could be as confident as he sounded.

'If you're sure. Look, I can cancel my plans for this afternoon, if you want to go for a drink or something.'

Seb—who was even more of a womaniser than he was a cynic—was offering to give up a hot date for him? Charlie's irritation at his younger brother suddenly melted, and he grinned. 'Watch it, Seb. You're beginning to sound a bit too much like me.'

'No chance. I don't have rose-tinted glasses,' Seb said, laughing back. 'I'll catch you later. If you change your mind, you know my mobile number.'

'Yes. Thanks.' Charlie replaced the receiver thoughtfully. No, Sophie wasn't walking all over him. She just needed some time. She'd call him later. He was sure of it. For now, he'd go for a walk. Clear his head. And maybe she'd call when he got back.

Thank goodness she was on a late shift, Sophie thought. It meant she had enough time to go home, shower, wash her hair, pour enough caffeine down her throat to steady her nerves, and be back to the white-coated professional everyone knew her as at the hospital.

Even without dark glasses, Sophie managed to avoid anyone's eyes on the way back to her flat by the simple strategy of keeping her gaze fixed to the ground and buying her tube ticket from the machine on the wall rather than the station clerk. But, despite the length of her walk, she was still no nearer knowing how to deal with this. What to say to Charlie. She'd made it even worse by running from his place without so much as a note.

'Talk about stupid,' she berated herself.

After her third cup of coffee—and knowing that she only had five minutes before she had to leave for the hospital—she summoned up the courage to ring Charlie. Their department protocol was that all senior doctors had the consultant's home number in case of emergencies. This wasn't an emergency, but it certainly wasn't a normal situation either.

She waited for him to pick up the phone. Maybe he was still asleep.

The answering-machine kicked in, with his familiar deep, posh voice. 'Sorry, I can't take your call just now. Leave a message after the beep.'

She froze. What the hell did she say now? Sorry I ran out on you? Sorry I waited until the moment your body was going to slide into mine and changed my mind? Sorry I ruined your night?

Nothing sounded right.

She took a deep breath, and was about to speak when there was a second long beep and the phone went dead.

Hell. He *would* have one of those machines that only gave you a limited time to record a message.

She couldn't bring herself to ring him again. And she would be late for work if she didn't get a move on.

Work. Was Charlie in today? As a consultant, he was probably off duty on a Sunday. Then again, he'd been in last night. Saturday night, the shift everyone hated working.

Well, she'd deal with it when she had to. Right now, she had a job to do.

To her relief, he wasn't at the hospital when she walked into the ward. She went through the handover, then checked on Lois.

'How are you feeling?' she asked.

'Scared. Sore.' Lois shuddered. 'I want to go home.'

'Home, or to a safe place?' Sophie asked gently. 'We can get the police to arrange it, if you'd feel safer somewhere else. Or maybe you've changed your mind about calling your parents?'

Lois shook her head. 'I told the police it was a stranger, someone I didn't know, but that wasn't strictly true.'

Statistics showed that most rapists were known to their victims, so Sophie wasn't that surprised. 'That's OK. Nobody's forcing you to tell anybody anything you don't want to. It's entirely your choice.'

'I want to ring my mum, but I can't. I just can't.' Lois wrapped her arms around herself. 'How can I tell her that she's going out with the man who did it?'

Lois's mum's boyfriend had attacked her? That explained why Lois had been so adamant that she couldn't ring her mother. Sophie sat on the edge of Lois's bed and put her arm around her. 'Do you have a brother or a sister? An aunt you could talk to?'

'Nobody. My dad's family never wanted to know us, my mum's an only child and so am I.'

'Best friend?' Sophie suggested.

Lois shook her head. 'I feel so dirty. I scrubbed myself in that shower. Several times. And I still don't feel clean.'

'It's not your fault,' Sophie reminded her.

'And my mum wouldn't believe me. He's probably told her I gave him the come-on, wearing short skirts and flaunting myself at him. She'll just think I'm trying to split them up because I don't like him.'

With good reason, Sophie thought bitterly. But she understood exactly how Lois felt. She'd been there. Had tried to tell the truth, and hadn't been believed.

'He's a lot younger than her. He's only ten years older than me. She'll blame me, say I was trying to take him from her.'

'Of course you weren't,' Sophie soothed. When Lois was calm again, Sophie looked at her chart. 'Last night, I was worried in case the bruising on your back was linked to kidney damage. The good news is, there aren't any traces of blood in your urine, so I'm pretty sure that everything's fine. The bruises should go down in a few days. If you want to go home, I can sign your discharge form—though you need to come back here and have your stitches removed by Charlie rather than go to your GP.' She knew that removal of the sutures was almost as crucial as placing them in the first place. If they were taken out badly, the scars would be worse. She sighed. 'I'd be a lot happier if you were going to stay with someone else.' If she let Lois go back to her own place, what was to stop the man who'd raped her from trying it again?

'There isn't anywhere.'

'Will you let me talk to the police?'

Lois shook her head. 'I can't testify. I can't.'

'You don't have to,' Sophie said gently. 'But they can find

you a safe place to stay. And they'll help you get your locks changed, that sort of thing.'

Lois's eyes looked haunted. 'In case he comes back?'

'They can do something. Get a court order to make him keep away from you. I don't know a lot about the law, but I'm pretty sure your mum doesn't have to be involved.'

Lois sucked in a breath. 'I…'

'Let them help you,' Sophie said. 'And you need counselling. I'll find the number for you.'

And maybe, she thought, it's time I called that number myself.

To her relief, Charlie wasn't on duty. And when she got home there was no message on her answering-machine. No note pushed through her door.

She ought to ring him and explain. It was the least she could do. But when she got his answering-machine message again, she cut the connection. This wasn't the sort of conversation she wanted to have with a machine. She needed to have it with Charlie himself. She sighed, then dialled another number. A call she should have made a long, long time ago.

The longer Charlie walked on the Heath, the more his worries surfaced. He'd assumed that Sophie's silence stemmed from embarrassment. Had he read it wrong? Was it really because she wasn't interested and he didn't mean that much to her? Was Seb right, and Charlie was just hopeless when it came to women, letting them walk all over him?

He'd certainly been wrong about Julia.

Maybe he was wrong about Sophie, too.

He checked his answering-machine when he got home. Two messages: one from Vicky—who'd clearly talked to Seb—and an earlier one where someone had obviously dialled a wrong number and hadn't hung up in time. No point in wondering if it had been Sophie. There was no message.

And she didn't call him later in the day either. Or that evening. Nothing but silence.

Facing her on Monday morning was tough. His body urged him to pull her into his arms and kiss away all the barriers between them. His mind knew better. So he simply nodded coolly at her, as if she were just another colleague at the Hampstead General. 'Morning, Dr Harrison.'

'Morning,' she replied, equally coolly.

The prickle of tension at the back of Charlie's neck turned to a burn as he realised what she'd just said. She hadn't even used his name. And her face betrayed no emotion whatsoever. Not a bloody thing. His stomach clenched as he realised that the doubts he'd had yesterday were more than justified. He'd been kidding himself, Saturday night really *hadn't* meant anything to her. She didn't care for him at all.

What an idiot he was. He'd sworn to himself that he'd never make the same mistake again. Never let himself be used, the way Julia had used him. And what had he just done? Lived up to his stereotype. Baron Charlie: 'fraightfully naice' but terribly dim.

Julia had used him to get herself the lifestyle she wanted. She'd wanted to be Baroness Radley, invited to all the best parties, with a name that would open any door. She'd just forgotten to inform him of the fact that she was in love with someone else. That she'd even been sleeping with that someone else up to the week before she'd planned to marry Charlie. Had he not found it out for himself in the cruellest possible circumstances, Charlie would never have believed it. He'd have been mug enough to marry Julia. And then he'd have had to plunge the family into debt to escape from the sham marriage.

His brother's words echoed in his head. *There's looking after, and there's being taken advantage of. You're such a soft touch...*

He'd been so sure that Sophie was different. But she wasn't. OK, so she wasn't a gold-digger, but she'd wanted something specific from him, too. She'd been upset on Saturday night—and he knew she'd been telling the truth about that. But, now he thought about it, maybe she'd thawed out towards him a bit too quickly. She hated upper-class men because she'd been hurt by them. She'd pigeonholed him along with the rest of them. On Saturday night she'd been prepared to make love with him. And now the agenda was obvious: upper-class twit hurts her, different upper-class twit heals her, all's right with her world.

'And you,' Charlie said savagely to himself as he closed his office door behind him, 'are most definitely an upper-class twit.'

From now on, things would be strictly professional between them. He'd definitely learned his lesson: twice bitten, always shy. The damned title would just have to pass to Seb or—since Seb probably wouldn't ever settle down and have kids—to another branch of the family. Because Charlie wasn't going to get married or have kids to saddle with it. Ever.

So much for caring. So much for wanting to make her feel better. She'd cried over him, she'd poured her heart out. And he hadn't even asked her how she was! OK, so she'd left without a word yesterday morning. But surely he was bright enough to realise that she'd just panicked?

Sophie's lip curled. No, she'd read it all wrong. All that had been between them had been sexual attraction. He'd realised that she was attracted to him. He'd been using her to scratch an itch—and she'd been stupid enough to let him do it.

It was like that postcard her friend Sandy had sent her from San Francisco, about what men said and what they really meant.

'I'm hungry.' Translation: I'm hungry.

'I'm tired.' Translation: I'm tired.

'Your dress looks nice.' Translation: I'd like to have sex with you.

'Do you want to dance?' Translation: I'd like to have sex with you.

'Would you have dinner with me?' Translation: I'd like to have sex with you.

She'd been amused by it at the time. But now it wasn't funny any more. It was too close to the bone. What had Charlie said? 'No strings... I'll just give you some space to be you.' Translation: I'd like to have sex with you.

How close she'd been to being *really* suckered.

She just hoped that nobody in the department would ever find out that she'd spent Saturday night in Charlie's bed. If they did, her life really wouldn't be worth living.

CHAPTER ELEVEN

FOR the first time in her entire career, Sophie didn't stay late after her shift or arrive early that week. She wanted to minimise the chances of having to see Charlie. They maintained a veneer of civility, but whenever she caught his eye in Theatre his gaze was ice-cold. It was obvious that he despised her. Whatever he'd said to her on Saturday night, he'd had time to think about it—and he'd obviously come to exactly the same conclusion as Sophie's tutor, all those years ago.

Well, she didn't care what he thought, she decided on Tuesday night when she knocked on the office door at the exact time for her appointment.

'Miss Harrison? I'm Melanie Bridges. Do come in.'

Melanie looked like everybody's favourite aunt. In her late forties, Sophie guessed. She had a kind face, and Sophie knew that anything she told Melanie wouldn't go any further. She was completely trustworthy.

Just what Lois needed.

And just what Sophie herself needed.

After they'd dealt with the paperwork and Melanie had given her a glass of water, it was crunch time.

Time to face up to her demons.

'Tell me about it,' Melanie prompted softly.

And Sophie began. She told Melanie everything she'd told Charlie. All her old feelings flooded back, the overpowering fear as they'd held her down and she'd realised how helpless she'd been. The shame at what had been happening. The disgust. The self-loathing. The nagging doubt that maybe, just maybe, it *had* been her fault. The way her tutor just hadn't believed her. And there was that itchy, tight feeling all over her skin, as if mud and slime had caked all over her and was glued fast and would never come off again.

Melanie sat there, not judging, just listening and handing Sophie a tissue when she needed one or topping up her glass of water after Sophie had tried unsuccessfully to swallow her emotions with her drink. A bitter pill that was too big, too difficult to swallow.

'And I'm the first person you've told?' Melanie asked, when Sophie had finished.

Sophie shook her head. 'Second.' In some respects, it was easier to talk about it for the second time. 'I don't want to bury it anymore, pretend it didn't happen.'

'Which is good. If you hide it, it'll just grow in the dark and that'll make it harder to deal with,' Melanie said. 'What we're going to do over the next few sessions is talk about how you're feeling, and work out between us how to help you cope with it. But the important thing you need to realise is that you weren't to blame for someone else's actions.'

Maybe. But there was one thing she was definitely to blame for. Running out on Charlie on Sunday morning. 'I want to deal with this,' Sophie said. 'I want to move past it. So I can get on with my life, have a proper relationship again.'

It was going to take time, but she was going to get over it properly. And maybe she'd even surprise her mum by dating someone and bringing him home to meet the family.

She squashed the name that came into her mind. No chance. She and Charlie Radley were history. *History.*

'I've got an unexpected cancellation tomorrow evening,' Melanie said. 'It's up to you if you'd like the slot. You might want to wait a week before you see me again.'

Sophie shook her head. 'No. I want the rest of my life to start as soon as possible.'

If only it could have been with Charlie.

But on Thursday morning she walked into the staffroom to be greeted with teasing smiles.

'Good morning, Baroness,' Sammy said.

'You kept that quiet, Soph. I thought you didn't even like the man.' Abby whistled. 'Well, I should've guessed you were protesting a bit too much.'

Sophie frowned. 'What are you talking about?'

Guy rolled his eyes. 'Stop playing the innocent. You and Charlie.'

'What?' Oh, God. They'd found out about Saturday night. But how? She hadn't told them. Surely Charlie hadn't. *Surely* he hadn't… 'There's nothing between me and Charlie,' she said, folding her arms.

'Nice try, Baroness,' Sammy said with a grin. 'But we've seen the pictures.'

'Pictures?' This had to be one of those weird realistic dreams, the sort where you were absolutely convinced everything was really happening because you were dreaming about people you knew. There weren't any pictures of her and Charlie…were there?

Without comment, Abby threw a magazine to her.

Acting on pure reflex, Sophie caught it.

'Page seven,' Abby said.

Ice trickled down Sophie's spine. This was a gossip magazine. There had to be some mistake.

It could only have taken seconds for her to flick to the page, but it felt as if everything was moving in slow motion.

And then she saw it.

A headline. CHARLIE IS HER DARLING!

A picture of Charlie helping her out of the taxi. He had his arm around her. He'd been *comforting* her—but it didn't look like that. It looked as if they couldn't keep their hands off each other.

Another picture, of the two of them going inside his flat.

And a picture of her, the morning after, letting herself out of his flat. Hair all over the place, because she hadn't been able to find her clip. Clothes rumpled, dark circles under her eyes. She looked as if she'd spent the entire night having sex with her secret lover.

She looked like a slut.

Horrified, she glanced through the text. It was all wild speculation about how long they'd been together and whether R. C. Radley, Baron Weston, would find true love this time with a workmate—surgeon Sophie Harrison.

And there was even a picture of her outside her own flat.

A photographer had been *spying* on her. Following her. And she hadn't had a clue.

Anger at the invasion of her privacy was mingled with fear. If she was that unobservant, anyone could follow her. She wasn't safe any more. Maybe she should start carrying one of those alarms that let off a deafening shriek at the pull of a cord—and keep it in her hand whenever she walked home.

'We've had four journalists on the phone already this morning,' Guy said quietly. 'We said you weren't in yet, and they asked for Charlie. He wasn't in either.'

'But…that's nothing to do with me!' Sophie stared at her colleagues—her *friends*—absolutely horrified. They thought she had spent the night at Charlie's flat? 'This isn't…' She couldn't get the words out; she could barely breathe, and her palms were sweating. 'This isn't what you think. It's…' Oh, no. She couldn't explain this. Not without going into things she'd wanted left private. 'It's not. It's just *not*.'

'Hey, we're all entitled to a fling,' Sammy said with a grin.

'I have *not* had a fling with him!' With shaking hands, Sophie flicked back to the cover of the magazine. Worse and worse. It was *Celebrity Life*. The magazine her mum always read. Which meant Sophie had a lot of explaining to do—and fast, before Fran saw it.

'Oh, God. I have to make a phone call,' she said, and rushed out of the room, not caring if they thought she was going to ring Charlie. She needed to talk to her mum. *Now.*

As soon as she was outside, she switched on her mobile phone and dialled her mum's number. Please, let Fran have her phone switched on. Please, please, please. She kept walking, ignoring the curious glances of people who passed her. They'd probably seen the pictures. They were probably thinking the worst. Oh, hell. She was going to have to have her hair cut short, dye it black and wear dark glasses for the rest of her life. And forget about her career—she could even hear a flushing sound as her plans all went down the toilet.

To her relief, her mother answered. 'Hello, love.'

Obviously her mother had recognised the number on the screen of her mobile phone as she'd answered it. 'Mum. Oh, thank God you're there.'

'Are you all right, Soph?'

'No. There's been a huge… Look, please, just don't buy *Celebrity Life* this week.'

'The issue with your picture in, you mean?'

She'd seen it already? Oh, no. Oh, no, no, no.

'The neighbours have been asking me about that.'

Fran's voice was even, but Sophie knew her mother well. She could hear the hurt that Fran was trying to disguise. 'Mum, it's not true.'

'That you're going out with a baron? It's your life, Sophie. You're an adult. It's up to you who you sleep with.'

'I didn't sleep with him!' Actually, she *had* slept with him. Just not in *that* sense. 'I didn't have sex with him,' she amended. 'Mum, it's not what it looks like. I swear.'

'I just wish you'd given us some warning, that's all. It's a bit embarrassing when people ask you if your daughter's going to have a posh wedding and what do they call her when she's a baroness.'

'Mum, just tell everyone it's a huge mistake and the papers have made it up.'

'Sophie, there are *pictures* of you.'

'I know. I've just seen them.' And she was still carrying the wretched magazine. Sophie gulped miserably. 'Mum, it's such a mess. What am I going to do?'

'What does he say about it?'

'Who?'

Fran sighed. 'Baron Radley, of course.'

'Oh, God.' She hadn't faced him yet. 'I...I'm going to have to talk to him. Mum, can I come round tonight? I don't want to talk about this on the phone.'

'You mean, in case someone's tapping it?'

Sophie hadn't thought of that. Could people tap your mobile phone? She cringed. Oh, the gossip magazines would have a field day with this if someone *did* tap her phone. 'Mum, I'll see you tonight. I'll tell you everything then.' Everything.

Including things she should have told her parents years ago. 'But if anyone asks you, just tell them it's not true. Please?'

'All right.'

'I love you. And Dad.'

'Is the baron coming with you?'

'No, he is *not*.'

'I see.' Fran's voice was slightly clipped.

Sophie sighed. 'Mum, it's not what you think. I'm proud of you and Dad. You've been the best parents anyone could ever ask for. I'm not asking him to come with me because *nothing is going on between us.* Believe me. I'll tell you everything tonight, I promise.'

'Ring me when you leave the hospital. I'll have dinner ready for when you get here.'

Despite her misery, Sophie smiled. Her mother's cure for everything: a good meal and a shoulder to cry on. And, boy, did Sophie *need* a shoulder to cry on right now.

Next step, Charlie. He wasn't in yet, and his secretary gave Sophie a distinctly speculative look.

Sophie decided to brazen it out. 'Could you ask him to page me in Theatre, please, when he comes in? It's urgent.'

'I see,' Marion commented, in a tone that said, *Are you going to have sex with him in the nearest linen cupboard then?*

Sophie sighed. 'Look, I realise half the hospital must have seen that magazine. But it's not how it looks. I need to see Charlie because I don't know how to deal with all this stuff, and he probably does. I'd appreciate if you could tell anyone who asks that I am not sleeping with Charlie Radley. He's not my type.'

'She's absolutely right,' a deep voice said behind her.

Oh, great. He *would* have to come in and overhear that last bit, wouldn't he? Things were bad enough between them without her insulting him as well. Sophie took a deep breath, and turned to face him. 'May I speak with you for a moment, please? In private?'

He gestured to his office. She walked in; he followed her and closed the door.

She'd heard the expression 'you could have cut the air with a knife', but this was the first time she'd ever experienced the feeling. Her skin felt too tight and it was hard to breathe.

'So. What can I do for you, Dr Harrison?' he asked coolly.

Kiss me better, a voice said in her head, and she felt her face heat. 'It's… Look. I'm sorry. About everything.'

Charlie supposed that was as near to an apology as he was going to get. Not that he wanted her to grovel. What he wanted was for her to get out of his office before he made a fool of himself and asked her to give him a chance, let him into his life.

She handed him a magazine. 'We have a problem. Page seven.'

When he reached the photographs and glanced through the text, he was very, very glad he'd kept himself in control. 'I see.'

She swallowed. 'Everyone's talking about us. The whole hospital. Everybody *knows.*'

'No, they don't. They just think they do.'

'How can you be so calm about it?'

'Because,' he said quietly, 'I've had to live with things like this for years.'

'It's horrible. There are journalists calling.'

He shrugged. 'Just doing their job. Following up a lead.'

'But they made all this stuff up. And they followed me home.'

There was the tiniest wobble in her voice: no doubt the thought of someone following her was bringing back memories of when someone else had followed her home.

Three of them.

He'd deal with this for her—but only because she was part of his staff. It had nothing to do with how he felt about her. He didn't feel *anything* about Sophie Harrison. Not one damn thing. Provided he didn't look into her eyes, or start thinking about how her hair had looked spread across his pillow, or remember how soft her skin felt. 'I'll sort it out. Refer all calls here to me,' he said coolly. 'At home, you might want to use an answering-machine for a while to screen your calls. It'll all die down in a few days when the next story breaks. In the meantime, it's a pain, but there's nothing you can do except ride it out.'

She nodded.

'And I'll speak to the department,' he said.

'Thank you.' She bit her lip. 'I'm sorry. About…' She took a deep breath. 'About Sunday morning.'

Me, too. Though he wasn't going to do anything about it. Keeping away from her was much, much safer. He could deal with being lonely. He was used to that. But he sure as hell wasn't going to get his heart broken again. Been there, done that—twice. Which only proved how stupid he'd been to fall in love with someone he barely knew. On impulse. Because of her glorious hair.

Well, not just her hair. Those beautiful eyes. The way she made a room light up. The way she had time for her patients, time to explain things to relatives, time to stand up for a junior doctor who was being bullied, time to make someone she barely knew feel better. The way she worked, deft and sure and meticulous. The way she caught her lower lip between her teeth when she was thinking.

And, heaven help him, he'd been stupid enough to fall in love with her. The force of the thought hit him as if he'd been punched in the stomach. He was in love with Sophie. A woman who couldn't care less about him.

How pathetic was that? He wanted to spend the rest of his life with someone who really, really wasn't interested in him. She'd even referred to the photographs of them together as 'a problem'—which made it very clear that she didn't want to be associated with him.

So he needed to fall *out* of love with her again.

Somehow.

'I'd better get to Theatre. I've got a full list.'

He nodded. 'Sure.' He clicked into his email, expecting her to leave.

'Charlie…'

He glanced up. She looked utterly miserable. As if there was so much she wanted to say, but she didn't even know where to start.

You and me both, he thought. But I'm not leaving myself open again. Not to you, not to anyone. He made his voice as cool and impersonal as he could. 'Yes?'

Defeat slunk into her face. 'Nothing.'

She probably thought he was the coldest, most callous bastard on the planet. Fine. Better that than knowing she'd put a crack through the centre of his heart. A crack that deepened every time he saw her.

He worked through his list of messages, ignoring the ones from the press and listing the others in order of priority. Then, when he judged that Sophie was safely in Theatre, he headed for the ward and called everyone into the staffroom.

'I believe most of you have heard rumours or seen the gossip rags,' he said. 'I'd just like to make it clear that the media will do anything for a great story. This isn't what it looks like. I'm not going to go into details—whatever Sophie has said to me remains confidential—but I'd like the rumours to stop. Sophie Harrison is my colleague. I value her in the same way that I value every single one of you: as part of the surgical team. I'm not sleeping with her or even going out with her. So I trust you'll join me in squashing any gossip in the hospital.'

There were several red faces, but a sharp glance from him had everybody nodding.

'Thank you. If any journalists start asking you questions, refer them to me. I'll deal with it. Now, I suggest we all get on with what we're paid to do. And, if I do hear any rumours, I'm fully aware of the disciplinary procedures in this hospital.'

Ignoring the look of surprise on people's faces—it was probably the first time any of them had heard him in high-handed alpha male mode—he turned on his heel and stalked back to his office. Problem solved. He hoped.

'Soph, stop playing with your sandwich and eat,' Abby said.

'I'm not playing with it,' Sophie lied. She didn't feel like eating. And everyone in the canteen was staring at her. She could feel their gazes burning into her skin.

'Yes, you are.'

'I'm going to shave my hair off and wear dark glasses,' Sophie muttered.

'Then people really *will* stare at you. Soph, you know what the grapevine is like. Tomorrow morning someone will have knocked you off top gossip spot. And Charlie made it very clear when he hauled everyone into the staffroom that nothing was going on between you. I think he'll scalp anyone who even whispers a rumour. He, um, mentioned disciplinary procedures.'

Because he hated the idea of his name being linked with hers. He'd been so cold to her this morning. As if a wall of ice was between them. It was obvious to Sophie that he really regretted what had happened between them. For him, it had been a moment's weakness.

She'd bared her soul to him, and he'd rejected her.

'Sophie? You didn't hear a single word I said, did you?' Abby asked.

'No,' Sophie admitted. 'Sorry.'

'I said, I feel bad about teasing you.'

'Why?' Had Charlie told the ward what she'd told him in confidence?

'Because—well, like I said, Charlie made it clear you just work together. I suppose it was a bit of wishful thinking. You'd be good together.'

'We most definitely would not,' Sophie said.

Abby opened her mouth as if to argue, but closed it again when Sophie glared at her.

'I'm going back to the ward,' Sophie said.

'Um.' Abby bit her lip. 'Sorry. I'll come with you.' She hurriedly finished her sandwich, and they left the canteen.

Sophie was still aware of people staring at her. She wished they'd stop. And, even more, she wished that she'd never met Charlie Radley.

Telling her parents the truth was even worse. Especially as she had to explain what had happened in Manchester all those years ago—although, thanks to Melanie, it was easier than it would have been before.

'Why didn't you tell us?' Sophie's father asked.

'Because you'd have made me pack everything up and come back home,' Sophie said. 'I wanted to finish my degree.'

'I could have made them admit the truth,' Sophie's father said, narrowing his eyes and bunching his fists.

'And ended up with a court case. Dad, it's the past.'

'Has this Charlie bloke laid a finger on you?'

Yes, but only because I begged him to. Sophie's face burned with embarrassment. 'Dad, he's a colleague. He's been a perfect gentleman.'

'So why were you sneaking out of his place on Sunday morning? Looking…well.' His mouth thinned. 'You know what you looked like.'

Sophie squirmed in her seat. 'Dad, I already told you that. I was upset, and he didn't want me to go home on my own. I stayed at his place.' Hopefully her father would think that meant 'spare room'.

'Leave her alone, Eddie,' Fran said. 'In fact, you can do the washing up while Sophie and I have a chat.'

'Mum, there's nothing else to tell you,' Sophie said when her mother directed her to the sofa and placed a large glass of wine in her hands.

'No? You're my daughter, Sophie. You've hardly had a boyfriend since you were a student. You said it was because you were too busy at work, though now I know what the real reason was. But you spent the night at Charlie's. So he means something to you, doesn't he?'

Sophie shook her head. 'Forget it, Mum. How is it ever going to work? We're from completely different backgrounds. He lives in the most expensive part of Hampstead and I live in the cheapest part. He's got a title—he comes from a small, refined family. Ours is noisy and messy and huge.'

At Fran's lifted brow, Sophie added, 'And I wouldn't swap a thing. What I'm saying is we move in different social circles. I wouldn't be comfortable with his lot, and he isn't used to our ways.'

'And have either of you tried?'

Sophie took a swig of wine. 'I met his sister. She's all right.'

'And you don't think he'd get on with us?'

'Mum, everyone gets on well with you.' She wrinkled her nose. 'Dad might be a bit funny towards him, though.'

'Because you're his little girl and he wants to protect you.' Fran hugged her. 'Except we failed you when you needed us. And your dad feels bad about that. So do I.'

Sophie shook her head. 'You didn't fail me because I didn't tell you.'

'We should have known.'

'You're not a mind-reader.'

Fran pounced. 'And neither are you. Why don't you give him a chance?'

'Who?'

'Don't play games with me, love. I'm your mother. You know who I mean. Charlie.'

Sophie willed her bottom lip not to wobble. 'Because I don't think he wants me.'

'Right. So the man sees you're upset. What does he do—ignore you? No, he takes you somewhere quiet, feeds you and gives you a place to stay. He cares all right.' Fran gave her a searching look. 'And I think I can guess what you didn't say in front of your father.'

'I didn't have sex with him!' Sophie said frantically.

Fran grinned. 'You're an adult, Soph. He's a nice-looking bloke. And a friendly hug doesn't always stay that way.'

Sophie buried her face in her hands. 'I can't believe we're having this conversation. You're my mother!'

'Who else are you going to talk to about it, love?'

She had a point. Sophie sighed. 'All right, I admit I stayed the night, but we didn't have sex. It didn't mean anything.'

'No? He's a baron, Sophie. He has the papers after him all the time. Would he really take you to his home—his private sanctuary—if you didn't mean anything to him?' Fran asked.

Sophie dropped her hands and looked at her mother. 'Mum, you're just being a romantic. This isn't going to have a fairy-tale ending. It's just going to be the most unholy mess. For weeks and weeks and weeks. I might even have to get another job.'

'Of course you won't. Things will calm down—by next Monday the hospital grapevine will be full of what someone else did on Saturday night. But Charlie took you back to his place. Think about what that really means,' Fran advised.

Sophie stared into her glass. 'There's something else. I made a total fool of myself, Mum. I cried all over him and he was so nice about it. Then I panicked the next morning when I woke up. I—Oh, God.'

'What did you do?'

'I left without saying a word to him.'

'Oh, Sophie. I never thought you'd be a coward.'

Sophie groaned and buried her face in her hands. 'I know. I feel terrible about it. But I just didn't know what to say to him. And it's too late now.'

'Not necessarily.' Fran waited a beat until Sophie uncovered her face again. 'He's The One, isn't he?'

Yes. Sophie tried to affect nonchalance. 'How would I know?' she asked, shrugging one shoulder.

'You just do, deep in your bones,' Fran said softly. 'He's The One. Otherwise you wouldn't have gone back to his place with him. You'd have made some excuse—at the very most, you'd have suggested a curry in a very crowded restaurant and made sure you got a taxi back to your place on your own afterwards.'

Which was exactly what she should have done. But she

hadn't. So was her mother right? Was Charlie The One? Was this why she felt so bad about it—why she couldn't get him out of her head?

'How did you know Dad was The One?' Sophie asked.

Fran smiled. 'I didn't even like him at first. I liked his friend. But his friend went off with my best friend, and we were stuck with each other. Our first date was a disaster. But I couldn't stop thinking about him. And I knew, the next time I saw him. I just knew I wanted to spend the rest of my life with him.'

'I can't stop thinking about Charlie,' Sophie admitted quietly. 'But when I spoke to him today… Mum, he was so cold.'

'Sounds to me like he was trying to protect himself,' Fran said. 'You must have hurt him when you didn't trust him enough to face him the next morning and talk about it.'

'Thanks, Mum,' Sophie said dryly. 'I feel bad enough as it is, without you piling on the guilt.'

'Then talk to him. You can't read each other's minds.'

'It's awkward.'

'Think about it,' Fran advised. 'If he's The One, nobody else is ever going to match up to him. Which gives you—ooh, I'd say, about half a century of being lonely. What's that, compared to a few minutes of awkwardness?'

Bleak, Sophie thought. Endlessly bleak.

'Talk to him,' Fran said again. 'Or you'll regret it. For the rest of your life.'

CHAPTER TWELVE

'CHARLIE made the gossip rags again this week, I see,' Seb said, pouring coffee into two mugs and handing one to his sister. 'Told you she was a gold-digger.'

Vicky rolled her eyes. 'You're such a cynic. And she's not a gold-digger.'

Seb snorted. 'Come on. Look at the pictures. And she isn't even that pretty.'

'If you weren't my brother,' Vicky said, 'I'd be sticking pins in you. I've met her, remember? And I don't see people through Charlie's rose-tinted glasses or your jaundiced yellow ones. She's OK.'

Seb's expression said what he thought of that one.

'And those photos didn't do her justice.'

Seb continued to look sceptical.

'Don't be so shallow. Looks aren't everything,' she berated him.

'No?' Seb grinned. 'You've led a sheltered life, Vic.'

Vicky scowled at him. 'If she wasn't in love with our brother, I'd be very tempted to set her up with you—so you could meet your match.'

'The woman who can match me doesn't exist,' Seb said with a shrug. 'Though I admit I'm having fun looking.'

'Oh, please. Spare me the details. You're horrible to women, Seb.'

'No, I'm not. I'm a realist. They know the score right from the start. I don't make any promises—so I don't break them either. And you love me anyway.' He opened a packet of chocolate biscuits and handed it to her, then dropped his teasing manner and looked serious. 'Are you sure she's in love with him, Vic?'

Vicky nodded. 'He matters. She doesn't want him to, but he matters. You'd have seen that if you'd looked at those pictures properly.'

Seb frowned. 'Seen what?'

'She'd been crying.'

'Because she found out he's got no money?'

Vicky slapped the back of his hand. 'Will you shut up about that, Seb? I already told you, she was going to flay him because she thought he was doing private nip-and-tuck jobs. Money doesn't bother her. She's got principles.' Vicky shook her head. 'There must be some kind of crossed wires between them.'

'And how are we going to uncross them?'

Vicky sighed. 'I don't know. I tried talking to Charlie this evening, and he told me to leave him alone. Actually, he had a bit of a hissy fit on me for going to the hospital to check her out.'

'He had one on me, too, for telling you about her in the first place,' Seb said. 'And Charlie doesn't have hissy fits. I think he's got it bad.'

'She's hurt him. Maybe we ought to pay her a visit.'

Seb choked on his coffee. 'Do you have any idea what that sounded like? Vic, you're seriously scary.'

His sister scowled at him. 'I didn't mean go and break her legs. She's not like bloody Julia.' They'd both wanted to murder *her,* and Seb had been the one to hold Vicky back. Just. 'I meant, so we can find out what's going on. He's not telling, so we'll have to ask her.'

'What makes you think she'd tell us anything?'

'You have a point. Women either faint at your feet or want to slap you—I think she'd fall in the latter camp. And she's not likely to talk to me because I gave her the once-over before Charlie had even had the chance to introduce her to us.' Vicky took another swig of coffee. 'Maybe we should get him plastered and make him spill the beans.'

Seb shook his head. 'Nice try, but you could pour a bottle of twelve-year-old malt down his throat and he still wouldn't tell. Charlie's a gentleman, in all senses of the word. He's too nice for his own good.'

'Maybe we should invite them both for dinner—separately—and then disappear and leave them to talk?' Vicky suggested.

'And what reason would she have to accept the invitation?'

'True.' Vicky folded her arms. 'We've got to do something, Seb. He's eating his heart out over her. And we're the only ones who can see it because everyone else believes the press image of Charlie, the debs' darling. They don't look any deeper.'

'We'll work on him first. Dinner,' Seb said. 'Saturday night.' Then he patted his chest. 'Ah, no, I can't. I'm working.'

'Tell her something's cropped up.'

Seb coughed. 'I meant, I'm on *duty*.'

Vicky grinned. 'Sorry.' There wasn't a trace of sincerity in the word. She knew her brother's womanising ways too well. 'Swap your shift, then. I'm sure you can talk someone into letting you owe them a favour.'

He raised an eyebrow. 'Being bossy, squirt?'

'Well, someone has to keep you two in line.'

Seb grimaced. 'And Mama dearest certainly isn't the woman to do it. OK, Vic. We'll take him out to dinner, pour a couple of bottles of Margaux down his throat and make him talk to us. Leave the booking to me. Somewhere quiet and discreet. I know just the place.'

'You,' Vicky said, taking another chocolate biscuit, '*would*.'

Where was the Director of Surgery when you wanted him? Sophie thought. Charlie seemed to have made himself completely scarce. He was always in a meeting, and when he wasn't either she was in Theatre or he was.

If she never saw him, how on earth was she going to talk to him?

Going to his flat uninvited wasn't an option. For all she knew, the paparazzi would follow her, hoping to get a story. Asking Marion for an appointment with Charlie also wasn't an option—she didn't want to give anybody any cause for gossip.

In the end she resorted to leaving him a message on his pager. 'Charlie, can we talk? Please?'

But either he didn't pick up her message or he didn't want to talk to her—because he didn't call her or try to see her. He didn't even email her.

So she had to face it. She'd blown it. He didn't want anything to do with her. And the fact that she couldn't get him out of her mind…well, that was her problem. She'd have to live with it.

Every day it took a bigger effort to walk into work. To pretend that everything was fine. To pretend she didn't notice that he was making himself scarce. Though at least the gossip about them had died down—some other scandal had knocked them off the hot topic list on the hospital grapevine.

Although one or two patients had given her strange looks

and actually asked, 'Aren't you the girl in that magazine—*Celebrity Life*?'

She'd pinned a smile she hadn't felt onto her face. 'I wouldn't know. I don't read those sort of magazines, I'm afraid.' And she'd switched the conversation back to post-operative care, discouraging any further discussion about the photographs.

She was coping, just, until she was paged by the emergency department. 'Soph? It's Paul. We've got a nasty for you. RTA. Child wasn't strapped in properly in the back, Mum had to do an emergency stop when a cyclist shot in front of her, and the child went straight into the back of the front seat. Pushed Gran through the windscreen. Baby didn't make it, Mum's got whiplash and is completely distraught, and Gran's in a bit of a mess—broken ribs, and I don't like the sound of her chest. I think she might have a ruptured diaphragm.'

A ruptured diaphragm was rare but could happen as a result of crush injuries—if the passenger had hit the dashboard on her way through the windscreen, the impact could have caused it. If left, the stomach would be strangulated. And if the herniation was massive, the resulting cardio-respiratory problems would get worse—and the patient could die. 'Done the X-rays yet?' Sophie asked.

'Waiting for them. Charlie's here, getting the glass out of her face and scrubbing it clean.'

Charlie. It would be the first time she'd faced him in a few days. Either he'd been in a meeting or she'd been in Theatre, and she had a feeling that he'd taken his lunch-breaks at his desk. Just as she'd taken as many of her breaks at her desk—her paperwork had never been this up to date.

And now she was going to have to work with him. She hated seeing that part of plastic surgery anyway—when they used a wire scrubber to get the dirt out to avoid tattooed scarring in the dermis. Seeing him would just make it worse. But she couldn't possibly leave the patient until he'd finished. 'I'm on my way.'

She stopped briefly to ask Sammy to alert Theatre, then headed down to the emergency department. A quick assessment of her patient—noting that she was in respiratory distress and there were definite bowel sounds in her chest—and a check of the X-rays told Sophie what she needed to know. 'Spot on, Paul. Ruptured diaphragm. And it's a big one. I need her in Theatre right now,' she told Charlie.

He shook his head. 'The quicker I get to work on these injuries, the better the results will be,' Charlie said.

'I need her in Theatre *now*,' Sophie repeated. 'She's got a ruptured diaphragm. The X-ray proves it—there's a linear split in the left diaphragm and her gut is herniating into her chest. Plus she's got broken ribs. It needs fixing before she arrests.'

'And I need to get this glass out of her face and clean it up. If I don't do it now, her skin will start to close and she'll have pitting and scarring. She'll end up being unable to bear the sight of her face in a mirror—and every time she sees those scars she's going to remember the accident and how her grandchild died. The chances are, she's going to blame herself for it—why didn't she make sure the child was strapped in properly, that sort of thing. So I'm not thinking of vanity here,' he said crisply. 'I'm thinking about potential psychological damage. Do you really think she needs a visual reminder of that loss every time she looks in a mirror?'

'She might not be alive to *see* her face if you don't let me get the rest of this sorted!' Sophie snapped.

He stared at her, a slight frown on his face, and Sophie flushed. Hell. She almost never lost her temper at work. And now here she was, yelling at Charlie. Add that to what had happened last week, and the hospital grapevine would be working overtime again.

'Compromise,' Charlie said quietly. 'We need to work together on this—I'm well aware of the medical risks of leaving it. Give me a couple more minutes to finish scrubbing and getting the glass out here in Resus, and I'll do the suturing in Theatre while you're repairing the diaphragm.'

'Right.'

She had one eye on her patient's monitors and one eye on Charlie as he worked swiftly, stopping every so often to assess the patient's skin colour.

But he still wasn't working fast enough. 'Charlie, I don't want her to arrest.'

'Will you stop nagging?' he asked through gritted teeth. 'I'm going as fast as I can.'

She shut up.

When they were finally in Theatre, she decided the best way through this was to pretend Charlie wasn't there and use this as a teaching session for Sammy. 'Sammy, ruptured diaphragms are quite rare. They're usually the result of a crush injury—typically from a car crash. I'm going to repair it abdominally for two reasons. Which are?'

'Because it doesn't tend to happen on its own and you want to check for any other organ damage.'

'Well done. It often occurs with a broken pelvis, but in this case the X-rays show we're OK. The most likely problems are a ruptured spleen—' the first case she'd worked on with Charlie. Not that she wanted to remember that right now '—and a ruptured liver. I hope it's not the liver, because if a hepatic tear extends to the cava we can end up with an air embolism. The other reason?'

'Not sure,' Sammy admitted.

'Because we're less likely to have pulmonary problems post-op,' she explained. She made the first incision. 'The liver's OK. That's good.' She sighed. 'But we have a damaged spleen. I'm going to do the diaphragm first so I've got room to work. The spleen isn't too bad, so I'll be able to glue it.'

She talked Sammy through the operation, explaining that she was extending the diaphragm rupture laterally so she could push the patient's stomach back into the abdomen. 'Next we wash out the chest. Why?'

'To avoid contamination from clots,' Sammy said.

'Spot on. Want to do it?'

Sammy nodded, and she supervised as he washed out the chest.

She repaired the laceration with continuous nylon suture. 'I'm putting stay sutures on either side to help tent the diaphragm downwards, because it helps with closure. You need to be careful here, Sammy. If the tear extends to the central tendon, there's a risk that you might catch the myocardium in it.'

She'd just finished suturing and was about to start repairing the spleen when the monitor beeped.

'Shit, she's gone into VF.' VF—ventricular fibrillation—was where the heart didn't beat properly, it just quivered. 'We need to shock her. You're not dying on me,' she told the patient as she prepared to use the defibrillator. 'Absolutely not. Your daughter's just lost her little one. She's not going to cope with losing her mum as well. We're going to get you through this. Charging to two hundred. And clear.'

Everyone stood back, including Charlie.

She placed the paddles on the old lady's chest.

'OK, sinus rhythm,' Sammy said.

First time. Lucky, but she couldn't take any more chances. She needed to work as swiftly as she could. 'We're there. BP OK?'

Sammy told her the readings.

'Good. Now for the spleen. I'm going to glue it.' She smiled at him. 'I know you've seen this before, so if you want to see what Plastics is doing—and Plastics doesn't mind being observed—that's fine.'

'Plastics,' Charlie said, his voice holding a noticeable chill, 'doesn't mind if Surgery doesn't. Sammy, if you stand here you'll get a better view.'

Sophie concentrated on gluing the spleen, but she was aware of everything Charlie was saying.

'With facial injuries, you can't use vertical sutures because you'd have to sacrifice too much viable tissue. So instead you use a large number of very, very fine sutures. What you need to do first with irregular wounds like these ones is to look for landmarks and match them—you're not wasting time by looking, because you don't get a second chance to do it. You look for two points that definitely fit, suture them together, and you'll find that more points fall into place: you suture them, and gradually fill in the bits in between. It's like putting together a very, very delicate jigsaw.' He sighed. 'With windscreen injuries, it's hard to get faces of tissue together that are exactly the same thickness. And we have to be very conservative about excising wounds—we need as much viable tissue as we can get. As it is, I'm probably going to have to do more surgery in a year or so's time—Z-plasty or dermabrasion.'

'Why are you using forceps and a curved needle and not a skin hook?' Sammy asked. 'I thought skin hooks caused less trauma to the wound margins.'

'They do—but they're slow, and we need to work as fast as we can,' Charlie said. 'With a curved needle you need to rotate your wrist so the insertion and pull-through point are in the line of the needle's curve. Just after you've sutured the wound there will be some oedema, so you need to take that into account when you're tying the sutures. If the knot's too tight, the suture cuts into the skin more rapidly and leaves a suture mark—that means a poor scar. And it's better to use interrupted sutures rather than continuous ones, because it gave a better cosmetic result.'

Sophie finished closing before Charlie was through.

'I'm going to see her daughter and give her an update on what's going on. Up to you if you want to stay,' she said to Sammy.

'Is that OK with you, Charlie?' Sammy asked.

'Sure.'

Charlie hadn't looked at her once, she noticed. Well, she could live with that. And she'd been snippy with him. Maybe they just needed to clear the air. She'd wait until he was out of Theatre, then tackle him.

Though it was easier said than done. When she did catch up with him and he turned to face her, his expression was completely unreadable. He may as well have still been wearing his surgical mask.

'I left you a message on your pager,' she said softly. 'A few days ago. Did you get it?'

His eyes glittered, just for a second. 'Yes.'

'Then…' He wasn't going to make this easy for her, was he? Then again, she hadn't exactly behaved well. 'Can we talk?' she asked. 'Not here, I mean.' Not where people could see what was going on and jump to wrong conclusions. 'Somewhere a bit quieter.'

He shook his head. 'There's no point. We have nothing to say to each other, Sophie. We're merely colleagues.'

People who had to work together and just lump it. He didn't even want to be friends with her any more.

'As you wish,' she said coolly, hoping that the misery weighing down the pit of her stomach didn't show in her eyes, and turned away.

There was nothing more to say.

Maybe it was time she started looking for another job.

CHAPTER THIRTEEN

'SO WHAT'S the occasion?' Charlie asked as he took his seat in the restaurant on Saturday night.

'Do we need an occasion to treat our beloved older brother to dinner?' Vicky asked.

He narrowed his eyes at her. 'Before you say anything, I don't want to discuss *that*.'

'Discuss what?' she asked sweetly. 'The venue? That's Seb's department.'

'You know exactly what I mean,' Charlie said warningly.

'OK, no discussion. I'll just tell you what we think, then. You need to find another girlfriend to take your mind off Sophie,' Seb said.

At Seb's grunt of pain, Charlie assumed that their sister had just kicked him under the table. Hard.

'What he means is, you're not happy,' Vicky corrected. 'We can see that. And we want to help.'

'Just stay out of it,' Charlie said tightly.

'Absolutely not. I've met her, remember. I liked her, and I think you'd be good for each other. You're obviously eating your heart out over her, and I reckon she's doing the same.'

Charlie looked away. 'I wouldn't know.'

'Well, we do. You've thrown a huge brick wall up. Just as

you did after She Who Must Not Be Named hurt you. Sometimes you can be too stubborn for your own good.' Vicky folded her arms. 'Have you discussed the problem with her, whatever it is?'

'No.'

'Why?'

'That's my business.'

'Er, no. This affects us, too,' Seb informed him. 'Neither of us likes seeing you unhappy.'

'Typical male,' Vicky said witheringly. 'You think women can read your minds and you don't have to tell them what you're thinking. Well, we can't. You need to talk to her, Charlie.'

'Is she on duty tonight?' Seb asked.

Charlie shrugged. 'How would I know?'

'Ring her, then, and find out. You do have her home number, I assume?' Vicky asked.

Yes. But he didn't think she'd speak to him. He leaned back in his chair. 'What's the point? I told her the other day that we had nothing to say to each other.'

'Which was very stupid of you. You'll just have to *unsay* it,' Vicky said.

'How?'

'Roses. Chocolates. Use your imagination. Oh, for God's sake, Charlie, stop being such a wimp. Just go and see her.'

'Right, and she'll really love having her pictures plastered everywhere again. Me with roses, her slamming the door in my face,' Charlie said wryly. 'I can see the headlines now. CHARLIE'S NOT HER DARLING.'

'Oh, stuff the paparazzi,' Seb said.

'Actually,' Vicky said thoughtfully, 'he's got a point, Seb. The media could screw this up, big time. What we need is a diversion. Then, while the paparazzi are busy with our little distraction, Charlie can leave quietly and sort things out with Sophie.'

'Hang on, I don't even know if she's at home,' Charlie protested.

The waiter came up and hovered discreetly by Seb. 'Are you ready to order, sir?'

'Can you give us another ten minutes, please?' Seb asked.

'Of course, sir.' The waiter nodded and went away again.

'Charlie, just go and see her. And if she's not there, you sit on her doorstep and wait until she gets home,' Vicky instructed.

'Who says I want to talk to her anyway?' Charlie asked, lifting his chin.

'You're in love with her. And don't pretend you're not— Seb and I have known you for our entire lives, and we know you better than anybody else,' Vicky said. 'And we think she's in love with you.'

Maybe she had been. But he'd blown that. 'She won't talk to me. Not now.'

'Charlie. Have faith in yourself,' Vicky said softly. 'Unless you try, you'll never know. You'll be miserable for the rest of your days and wonder what would've happened if you'd been brave enough to let her into your life.'

'I'm not a coward,' Charlie said through gritted teeth.

'So prove it.'

'And if she knocks me back?'

'Then at least you know where you stand. And you can move on—eventually.' She smiled at him. 'Go and see Sophie, while Seb and I create a diversion.'

'Oh, no. You're not going to take your dress off and dance on a table while you swig champagne out of the bottle, are you?' Seb asked, looking faintly worried.

Vicky folded her arms and gave him a pointed look. 'No, because *I'm* not the wild child of the family.'

'Don't look at me. I don't dance on tables, topless or otherwise,' Seb said.

'No, you're going one better than that.'

The worry on Seb's face deepened. 'Meaning?'

Vicky grinned. 'You, Sebastian, dearest, are going to be sold.'

'*What?*'

'For charity. Promise auction—and you're the star prize.'

Seb held both hands up. 'Wait a minute. What promise auction?'

'The one,' Vicky said sweetly, 'that you're going to arrange. A hospital fundraiser. A *big* one.'

Seb's jaw dropped. 'I can't arrange something like that!'

'Yes, you can. I might even help you, if you ask me nicely. And we're going to start the PR for it tonight—by giving *Celebrity Life* a scoop. All it takes is one phone call and they'll be here, dying to photograph you and find out as many details as possible. Meanwhile, Charlie slips out the back way, unnoticed, and can go to see Sophie without having the press in tow.' She winked at Charlie. 'Go get your girl, big brother.'

'Yeah,' Seb said, curling his lip. 'And if I'm going to put myself through a media circus for you, you'd better do it right. I'm accepting nothing less than the best man's job. And if you're lucky I won't leave you naked and tied to a lamppost on your stag do.'

'Hang on, who said anything about marriage?' Charlie asked.

'Rupert Charles Radley, this is the love of your life we're talking about. Of course you're going to get married,' Vicky said with asperity.

'Oh, and before you go.' Seb took his wallet from his pocket, rummaged inside and discreetly palmed something over to Charlie.

'Sebastian Henry Radley, if that's what I think it is… Do you have to reduce *everything* to sex?' Vicky asked.

He spread his hands. 'Just being practical. If we're talking kiss and make up, he needs to be prepared. Don't you start living up to your namesake, queenie.' He wrinkled his nose at her. 'Anyway, you're the one who's selling me for a night, so I don't think you have room to talk about reducing everything to sex.'

'You,' Vicky said, 'are impossible.'

'Agreed. But thanks. Both of you,' Charlie said, hugging his siblings.

'Go get your girl,' Seb told him. 'We have work to do.'

Vicky took her mobile phone from her handbag. 'OK. Round One of *Celebrity Life* versus the Radleys.' She grinned. 'Though it's going to be a knockout. They don't stand a chance against us!'

'Sophie? Is that you?' Mrs Baker poked her head round her door. 'Ah, at last.'

Sophie looked at her landlady in surprise. 'Is something wrong, Mrs Baker?'

'No, no. I've been entertaining your visitor.'

'Visitor?' Sophie echoed. She wasn't expecting any visitors. Unless Sandy had come home unexpectedly from her round-the-world trip… No. Sandy would have sent her a text or phoned her from the airport.

'There you go, young man.'

Young man?

Mrs Baker ushered Sophie's visitor out of her own door and into their shared lobby, and Sophie's heart missed a beat. Charlie. What was *he* doing here?

'Thank you for looking after me, Mrs Baker,' Charlie said. To Sophie's disgust, he actually gave a half-bow, raised Mrs Baker's hand to his lips and kissed it.

Her landlady turned bright pink and giggled. 'Oh, Charlie, you are a one!' She gave them both a coy little wave and closed her door.

'What do you want?' Sophie asked, knowing she sounded ungracious but not able to prevent it.

'To talk to you.'

She curled her lip. 'I thought we had nothing to say to each other? That we're "merely colleagues".'

'I was wrong,' Charlie said quietly. 'I think we have a lot to talk about. And I'd rather we said it somewhere a little more private.'

He had a point. Mrs Baker, bless her, probably had her ear jammed to the door—ready to come out to the rescue, brandishing her umbrella, if Charlie appeared to be upsetting Sophie. Worse, she'd be reporting back to Sophie's mother. Sophie gave in and opened her front door, letting him walk up the stairs first.

'I brought you these. Sort of a holding place, you might say,' Charlie said as she closed the door behind them, handing her a dozen multicoloured roses wrapped in supermarket Cellophane. 'There aren't any proper florists open at this time of night. I intend to give you a decent peace offering later.'

'I don't want flowers.' She'd just wanted him. And what a mistake that had been.

He sighed. 'I think we've made a mess of things between us. I'm sorry. I didn't give you a chance when you wanted to talk to me. I can't really expect you to listen to me now. But I'm asking you anyway. Can we talk it over?'

Sophie rubbed a hand across her eyes. 'I don't know what to say.'

Just then Charlie's stomach rumbled. Loudly.

He winced. 'Sorry.'

'How long were you waiting for me?'

'Since half past seven,' he admitted.

'So you haven't eaten tonight?'

He shrugged. 'Doesn't matter.'

She switched the kettle on and gestured to him to take a seat at her kitchen table. 'I'm not offering you a meal.' Even though she'd been brought up to be hospitable. When she and Charlie ate together, it…well, it *led* to things.

'I don't expect you to feed me.'

She sneaked a glance at him. He looked absolutely sincere. So maybe he really did just want to talk. And no doubt Mrs Baker had been grilling him for the past couple of hours while Sophie had been doing her handover and finishing some paperwork. She wouldn't have let him anywhere near Sophie if she didn't trust his motives.

And if he'd missed his evening meal to wait for her, she couldn't starve the poor guy.

'There's one of my mum's cakes in that tin,' she offered gruffly.

'Thank you,' he said quietly.

She handed him a knife and a plate, put the roses in water, pulled the blind at the kitchen window then turned to face him. 'So. What was it you wanted to say?'

This was it. His one chance. And he'd better not blow it. 'It's a long story. But, firstly, I want to apologise. I haven't treated you very well.'

'I haven't treated you very well either,' Sophie admitted.

'None of this was supposed to happen.' He sighed. 'I wasn't supposed to fall in love with anybody. Ever again.'

'Again?'

'I was engaged five years ago. Her name was Julia. She worked for an art gallery—her mother knew mine socially. Anyway, we went out together a few times. I thought I was in love with her.' And that she'd be the one to keep his mother off his back, an acceptable bride for the lord of the Weston estate. 'I asked her to marry me. She said yes.'

'So what went wrong?'

'She forgot to tell me,' Charlie said dryly, 'that she was in love with someone else. I thought she didn't mind me working doctor's hours because she knew how much my job meant to me. But, of course, it gave her a lot of free evenings.'

Sophie's eyes widened. 'She was seeing someone else behind your back?'

He nodded. 'I found out the hard way. I had a key to her place. The week before the wedding I thought she seemed rather stressed. So I planned a surprise for her. I was going to make her a special meal, give her a massage—you know the sort of thing. I took a half-day and went to her place early to set it all up.' He looked away, unable to bear seeing pity in Sophie's face when he told her. 'But she was already home.' He still remembered walking in. Hearing her laugh. Hearing the laugh turn to a cry—a cry he recognised. The cry of Julia climaxing. He still remembered being frozen at first, not wanting to believe it. She couldn't be unfaithful to him. She'd said she *loved* him. And then he'd forced himself to walk towards the bedroom door. One foot in front of the other. Mechanically. Opened the door. And seen them together. 'She was in bed. With him.'

'You walked in on them?'

'Yes. He was an artist. Not a very successful one. Still isn't.' He gave a mirthless laugh. 'Not that *that* matters. She met him at the gallery. But he couldn't give her the life she wanted, with invitations to all the smartest parties and people falling over themselves to know her. Whereas I could.' He felt a muscle flicker in his jaw. 'So she decided to have the best of both worlds. The position I could give her as Baroness Radley—and the lover she wanted on the side. And if I protested, she could always divorce me—a settlement would probably have been enough to set up both of them for life.'

'That,' Sophie said tightly, 'is appalling. No wonder your sister checked up on me. I take it you cancelled the wedding?'

'Yes. And I made it very clear to anybody I dated afterwards that I wasn't looking for marriage or any kind of permanent relationship.' He smiled wryly. 'You probably won't believe me, but most of the dates I had…I didn't even kiss them. Once bitten, twice shy, and all that. Half the time I didn't even want to go, but Seb was insistent that I shouldn't stay in and brood over Julia. He said I wasted all my opportunities.' He shrugged. 'I was more interested in my work. And then I came to the Hampstead General and met you.' He toyed with the cake. 'I never believed in the so-called *coup de foudre*—love at first sight—so I really wasn't prepared for feeling as if someone had dropped me out of a plane without a parachute. I couldn't take my eyes off you. But the second you looked at me your eyes were filled with loathing. I had no idea what I'd done to upset you.'

She shook her head. 'It wasn't you.'

'Just what I stood for. And if I'd been you, I would have reacted the same way.' He looked bleakly at her. 'Every time I saw you I just wanted to pull you into my arms and kiss you. It drove me crazy—I just don't *do* that sort of thing! And you'd put up this huge wall between us—it was if you could barely stand being in the same room as me.'

'And then I saw you looking so unhappy. Your heart-strings case.'

'Yes. That.' He crumbled a bit more of his cake. 'Let's just say that I don't get on that well with my stepfather.'

'He hurts your mother?' Sophie queried.

'If he did, I'd take him apart. Slowly.' And very, very painfully. Charlie flexed his hands, letting his fists unbunch. 'No, he doesn't hit her. He didn't hit any of us when we were growing up.' He smiled wryly. 'Mainly because we're all bigger than he is. He's just…tiresome, I suppose. I don't know if he thought he'd get a title if he married my mother. He certainly likes to pretend he's the baron. Though he's not fit to lick my father's shoes.'

'I'm sorry,' Sophie said softly.

'Not your problem. But the night I first kissed you… Ah, hell. There isn't a good way to put this.' If he said what was in his head—what was in his heart—she'd throw him out.

'Try the straight way,' Sophie suggested.

His eyes met hers. 'You're not going to like this,' he warned.

'Tell me anyway. I think it's time we were completely honest with each other.'

More than time. 'I knew I'd fallen in love with you. It was like nothing else I'd ever known. I thought I'd loved Julia, but that was a pale imitation of what I felt for you. I'd watched you on the ward: you were a bright light that brought everyone round you. The way you smiled, the way you had patience with junior doctors, the way you argued passionately for what you believed in and stood up against anything you saw that was wrong. You were just so warm and vital. So when I saw you so upset that night, I wanted to make you better. I wanted to bring the light back to your eyes. And I made a complete mess of it.'

She shook her head. 'No, you were brilliant.'

'Then why did you walk out on me without a word?'

She was silent.

Was she going to tell him? Or was she going to ask him to leave?

Eventually, she looked at him. 'I panicked,' she said softly. 'The next morning, the more I thought about what had happened, the less I could bear to face you. I'd led you on and I'd made you stop at the last moment. I mean, you must have been…frustrated.'

'I understood, Sophie. It wasn't just about sex—otherwise I'd have put you in a taxi that night and not asked you to stay with me.'

'Which only made it worse. You'd been so *nice* about everything. I'd cried all over you, I'd left you unsatisfied, I'd… Oh, I just wanted to crawl away into a corner and lick my wounds. I was ashamed, embarrassed. I didn't know what to say to you.'

So she'd said nothing. Left him in limbo. 'You could have left me a note.'

'I didn't know what to say,' she repeated.

'I guessed you'd felt embarrassed and upset,' he admitted.

'So why didn't you give me a break?'

He sighed. 'I tried not to pressure you. I waited for you to ring me. But the longer you left it, the more I started remembering what had happened with Julia.' He looked away. 'Let's just say I have trust issues. I talked myself into thinking that I'd read you wrong, that I didn't mean anything to you.'

'It wasn't like that. You were the first person I'd told about it, and I was still so churned up inside. I'm sorry I hurt you. I didn't want that to happen.' She swallowed. 'I thought you'd changed your mind about me, too.'

'Bluff,' Charlie said.

'Vicky said you were good with smoke screens.' Her face became more serious. 'I talked to Lois the next day. I persuaded her to talk to a counsellor. And…' she closed her eyes for a moment '…I rang the number, too.'

'You've talked to someone?'

She nodded. 'Her name's Melanie. I've seen her a few times, actually. And it's helped. A lot.'

'Good.' Lord, how he wanted to reach out and take her hand. Comfort her. But holding her hand was probably a move too far—he didn't want her to throw him out. Not until they'd said all they needed to say.

He resumed playing with the cake. He needed to keep his fingers busy before they turned traitor and followed his heart instead of his head. Before he touched her.

'I told my parents,' she said quietly. 'They were pretty upset. Dad felt he'd failed me because he hadn't protected me, and Mum felt she'd failed me because I didn't trust her enough to tell her. But if I'd told them, it wouldn't have made any difference.' She grimaced. 'You can't change the past. I just didn't want them to be hurt.'

'And then they saw those pictures in *Celebrity Life*. I imagine your father doesn't feel very kindly towards me either,' Charlie said.

'Mum talked him round. I, um, told her most of what happened. She said I ought to talk to you.' She waited a beat. 'I tried.'

He remembered. 'And I wouldn't let you.'

'Because I'd hurt you.'

'As I just told you, I…' He sighed. 'I find it hard to trust since Julia. And with everyone else seeing Baron Radley instead of Charlie, wanting what they can get out of me…I talked myself into thinking that you'd just used me. That you were getting your revenge on an upper-class twit. That, like Julia, you hadn't wanted me for myself. Just for what I represented.'

'No. It wasn't like that.' She took a deep breath. 'I was just being a wimp.'

'Wimp,' he said slowly, 'is the last word I'd use to describe you. You've got guts, Sophie Harrison. And I respect you.'

'I respect you, too. Professionally and personally.' She paused. 'What would you have done if I'd stayed that Sunday morning?'

'Bearing in mind that I could sleep through an earthquake…when I'd finally surfaced, I would've made you breakfast in bed and tried to persuade you to talk to a counsellor.'

'Really?'

'If you'd been awake, yes.' The other thing he'd wanted to do must have been written all over his face. Well, now was the time for honesty. He may as well tell her. He had nothing left to lose. 'If you'd been asleep, I might have woken you with a kiss. Seen where it took us.'

'I thought you'd just wanted me to…well, scratch an itch.'

'No. Though I admit I wanted to make love with you. I still do,' he admitted. It was taking all his willpower to keep him on his chair. What he wanted to do right now was to scoop her up and sit her on his lap and kiss her. And more. Until they both felt a hell of a lot better.

Though now wasn't the time. They needed to talk things through. 'But I want more than sex.'

Very quietly, as if she was afraid of the answer, she asked, 'Which means what, exactly?'

'I want to spend the rest of my life with you. Though I have certain obligations,' he warned, 'so I can't promise you a rich life.'

She coughed. 'Says the man who lives in a posh flat in the most expensive part of Hampstead.'

'It's not mine,' he said. 'Well, it *is* mine, but it's part of the Weston estate. I can't sell it and bank the profits. And most of my salary goes to prop up the estate. Old houses just *eat* money. They need things done to them, and you wouldn't believe how many regulations there are about building work. All of which adds to the cost of the remedial work—the right materials, the right craftsmen and the right method, not to mention fitting in with modern planning regulations.'

'Money doesn't bother me.'

'I know. Vicky told me.' He smiled wryly. 'After I'd threatened to scalp her for giving you the once-over.'

'Obviously she just wanted to make sure I wasn't another Julia.'

'You're not.'

'But I don't come from your world, Charlie. I come from the East End. My family isn't posh. What you see is what you get.'

'Which is fine by me. Actually, I envy you your family. It must be nice to know that people love you just for yourself.'

'But your family love you for yourself.'

He shrugged. 'Seb and Vicky do, yes.'

'And your mother?'

Charlie chose his words carefully. 'Appearances are important to her.'

Sophie made the leap instantly. 'So she won't approve of me.'

Charlie made a face. 'You don't need her approval. I make my own decisions. But I can't offer you a normal life, Sophie. Because of who I am, people are always going to be interested in what I do. And the gossip rags will speculate when there isn't a story, just to keep things ticking over. When are we getting married? Are you pregnant? Am I having an affair? Does one of us drink too much or take Prozac?' He sighed. 'Be with me, and you'll be in the public eye, too. And our children— heaven help any of them if they try to sneak into a nightclub or a bar under age. There'll be photographic evidence, they'll be labelled as wild socialites and we'll be pilloried as terrible parents who have no control over their kids.' He crumbled the last piece of cake. 'I saw how those photographs in *Celebrity Life* upset you. I won't ask you to give up your privacy for me.'

'So where does that leave us?'

The first glimmer of hope lightened his heart. She thought there was an 'us'? 'I'll get the lawyers onto it.'

'Onto what?'

'How I can stop being Baron Radley and become just Charlie. And when I can offer you an ordinary life, I'll ask you to share it with me. As my wife. My equal partner.'

There was a long, long pause. Charlie's heart started beating faster. Was this it? Was this the moment when she told him she didn't want to share his life, regardless of who he was?

'Remember what you said to me in the emergency department? Compromise,' she said softly. 'You don't have to give up being Baron Radley. And what does the "R" stand for, anyway?'

'Rupert. After Prince Rupert of the Rhine.' He grimaced. 'I've used my middle name since the second day of school— no way was I putting up with any more teasing about whether my surname was Bear and if I had yellow trousers with big squares on them.'

She laughed. 'Sorry. But I can just imagine you as a four-year-old, scowling at everyone who called you Rupert the Bear. Do I take it you hate a certain Elvis Presley song, too?' She hummed the first couple of lines of 'Teddy Bear'.

'I wish I hadn't told you now,' he muttered.

'I promise not to call you Rupert. Though it's not *that* bad.' There was a wicked gleam in her eyes. 'I mean, your parents could have called you Bradley. Imagine being called Bradley Radley.'

'Oh, please.' He shuddered. 'And what did you mean, I don't have to give up being Baron Radley?'

'Being a baron gets you free theatre time in Harley Street. Time you use to help people. Giving up being a baron means you won't be able to do that, because you won't have your bargaining tool any more,' she pointed out. 'And you'll hate not being able to make a difference.'

How did she know him so well, so soon?

He realised he'd spoken aloud when she said softly, 'I just do. Because it was the same for me. I didn't want to fall for you. You stood for everything I hated—you're posh, you're upper-class, you're so very confident. Except, time after time, you proved me wrong about you. You back your staff, you make sure the junior doctors are looked after properly, you care about your patients.' She paused. 'I'm scared, Charlie. I'm scared I'm not going to live up to what you want.'

'Sophie, you already do,' he said simply.

'I don't mean that. I mean…' She stopped, and sucked in a breath.

He knew exactly what she meant. 'Sex.'

CHAPTER FOURTEEN

'SEX.' How could such a little word be so—well—huge? Sophie thought.

'I'm going to ask you an embarrassing question, if I may,' Charlie said.

She had a pretty good idea what he was going to ask. And trust Charlie to be polite about it.

'Have you made love since you were attacked—apart from that night with me, I mean?' he asked softly.

'I've had boyfriends,' she said defensively.

'That isn't what I asked.'

She stared at the table. 'No. I haven't.'

'Sophie. If this is going to happen, you have to trust me,' he said, his voice gentle. 'We started making love. When we were face to face, side by side, it was fine. You were responding to me. It was working.'

'Do you *have* to analyse it like this?' she muttered.

'Hear me out,' Charlie said. 'I think I know when you got scared. It was when I leaned over you—because it reminded you of being pinned down.'

Sophie forced herself to breathe evenly. 'Yes.'

'So. I have a theory.' He smiled at her. 'Want to test it?'

'Yes. And no. I'm scared,' she admitted.

'Sophie, I promise I'll never hurt you. Any time you want to stop, we'll stop,' he said. 'No pressure.' He shifted in his chair and held his arms out.

So she was going to have to learn to trust him with herself. Trust him not to hurt her. Trust him to wipe the bad memories away. Let him finish the healing process that had begun with her counselling.

Slowly, she stood up. Walked the six steps from her side of the table to his. Let him pull her onto his lap.

'It's not so bad, is it?' he asked softly, nuzzling her cheek and sliding his hands round her waist.

She put her hands round his neck. 'No.'

'Kiss me, Sophie.' He tilted his head back, offering his mouth to her. His blue, blue eyes invited her to blow his mind.

Just like he blew hers.

She bent her head. Brushed her lips against his, very lightly. His hands tightened slightly against her waist, then relaxed. 'Sorry.'

He wanted more—she could tell by the need in his eyes. But he was trying so hard to keep within her comfort zone, not push her back into being scared. She reached back and removed the clip from her hair. He took a sharp intake of breath as her hair fell over her shoulders. 'Oh, God. Your hair drives me crazy.'

'Good,' she said with a grin. She bent her head again and nipped at his lower lip with hers, teasing him until he opened his mouth and let her explore him.

Kissing was good. Very good. She could kiss him for hours. His mouth was soft and sweet and teasing, and he was letting her set the pace.

More? Yes, she wanted more. He was wearing a black round-neck cashmere sweater—it felt glorious, soft and warm against her fingers, but she wanted the touch of his skin. She tugged at the hem, then slid her hands underneath, smoothing them over his abdomen.

His breath hissed. 'Sophie.'

'I want to touch you,' she whispered. 'And, nice as your sweater is, it's in the way.'

'So what do you want to do about it?'

'I want you to raise your arms,' she said.

His pupils widened as he realised what she was intending to do, and he raised his arms. She eased his sweater up and over his head, then folded it neatly.

'What?' she asked, catching his grin.

'You can tell you're a surgeon. You're very neat.'

'And what would you have done? Dropped it on the floor?'

'Let's see. The choice is, be prissy about my clothes or have your hands on my body.' He drummed his fingers on his chin. 'Yes, I think the sweater hits the floor. Who cares about crumpled clothes?' He smiled at her. 'But tonight we'll do it your way. I'm all yours, Sophie. Do what you want with me.'

Pleasure thrilled through her. 'Whatever I want?'

'Whatever you want,' he promised.

'Mmm.' She ran her hands over his torso. 'You feel good, Charlie.'

'Kiss me again?' And it was a plea, not a demand.

She did. But it wasn't enough. She needed more. She wanted them to be skin to skin.

'Touch me, Charlie,' she whispered.

'You're wearing too much.'

'Take it off.'

He shook his head, holding her gaze. 'No. Because then it's my choice to remove your clothes. Tonight, it's your choice. You're in control.'

Suddenly she understood what he was doing. All those years ago, the choice had been taken from her. Tonight, he was giving it back.

'I don't want to get undressed in my kitchen. Even though the blind's drawn,' she added.

'Then what do you suggest?' he asked softly.

In answer, she slid off his lap and held her hand out. He took it, and she pulled him to his feet. 'Come with me.'

Charlie had to use every ounce of control not to pick her up and carry Sophie to her bedroom. He'd done that before—albeit he'd carried her to his bed, not hers—and it had all gone wrong. This time they'd do it her way. So she felt safe. And then, maybe, they'd both get what they wanted. Each other.

He followed her to her bedroom. It was just what he'd expected: the room was small, painted a bright sunny yellow. The double bed had an iron frame, and the duvet cover and pillows were in a lighter shade of yellow. There was a pile of books—medical books, by the look of them—on the bleached pine cabinet next to her bed and a wrought-iron lamp with a cream shade on it.

Sunshine. Just like her hair. Like Sophie herself.

'Do you ever just wear jeans and a sweater?' she asked.

He looked down at his trousers. 'What's wrong with these?'

'Nothing. But they're designer.'

He sighed heavily. 'For your information, they were a present. From my mother. Because the gossip rags caught me in some very disreputable jeans a couple of years back.' He rolled his eyes. 'I'd been doing some maintenance work on the flat, I'd run out of biscuits, and I wasn't going to bother changing out of my work gear for the five minutes it'd take me to nip to the local shop for supplies. They ran a story speculating about whether I'd lost all my money at an online casino.'

Sophie chuckled.

'It wasn't funny at the time. You wouldn't believe the lecture I got about my clothes. Anyone would've thought I was fourteen, not thirty-four.'

It was a stupid story. But it had made her laugh, broken the tension he'd seen building in her eyes.

Then she stopped smiling. 'So what were you wearing underneath your jeans?'

'The same sort of thing that I'm wearing now.'

'Show me,' she said, her voice a husky whisper.

She wanted him to take his clothes off? Oh, yes. Please. On the other hand, if he stripped off it would leave her in no doubt about just how aroused he was. He didn't want to scare her again. 'Are you sure?'

'Oh, yes.'

Slowly—hoping she wouldn't see that his hands were shaking—he unbuttoned his trousers. Let them fall to the floor. Kicked them aside, managing to nudge off his socks at the same time—socks just weren't sexy.

'OK?' he asked.

'Very OK.' She walked over to him. 'But this, I think, is my job.' She hooked her fingers into the waistband of his grey marl jockey shorts and slowly drew the fabric downwards.

Charlie closed his eyes. He counted backwards from a hundred—in sevens. Thought about different types of sutures. Anything to stop him doing something stupid, like grabbing Sophie and kissing her senseless.

He had to take this slowly. At her pace. Even though every single cell in his body was going crazy with desire for her.

'You're beautiful,' she said, and her voice was shaking.

Charlie opened his eyes. 'Sophie? Are you all right?'

'I think so. But you're so beautiful.' She trailed her hand across his ribcage. 'I want a picture of you. Just like this.'

'Watercolour, oils or photograph?'

She grinned. 'Just as long as the original's mine.'

'Oh, it is.' If she didn't touch him again—and soon, and a lot more intimately—he was going to dissolve. It was hard to breathe. And even harder to stop himself grabbing her. He resumed counting backwards—this time from a thousand, in seventeens.

'What are you doing?' she asked.

'Huh?'

'You've got this weird look on your face.'

He told her.

She frowned. 'Why?'

'So I can keep my control. So I don't just grab you and make a mess of this. But I think, if you don't touch me soon— if I can't touch *you* soon—I might just expire.'

'Ah, yes. The small matter that you're naked, and I'm fully clothed.' She gave him the wickedest grin he'd ever seen, and his temperature rose another notch. 'Sorted.'

She stripped. In six seconds flat. And he knew that, because he was counting.

He held his arms wide, and she walked into his embrace. He didn't dare wrap his arms round her. He just kissed her, and hoped she could tell from the heat of his mouth just how much he wanted her. Desired her. Needed her.

Loved her.

All he was aware of was Sophie. Her scent, the warmth of her skin, the softness of her hair. The way her mouth responded to him, teasing him. The way the tips of her breasts brushed against him, making his body tighten even more. And then, somehow, they were on her bed. Lying facing each other, on their sides.

'You're so beautiful,' he whispered. 'Such incredible curves.' He drew one hand down her side, palm flat and stroking along the dip of her waist, the arch of her hip. 'And I could drown in your eyes. And your mouth—oh, even thinking about your mouth makes my synapses stop working properly.'

'Yeah?'

'Yes.' His breath hissed from him as Sophie copied his actions, moulding the curve of his buttocks.

'I want to make love with you, Charlie.'

'It won't be just sex,' he warned her. Because he wouldn't be making love only with his body. His heart would be right there, too. And his soul. And he really, really hoped she knew that. He really, really hoped it'd be the same for her, too.

He kissed her again, then drew a line of kisses down her neck, across her collarbones. When he wriggled lower to take one nipple into his mouth she gave a sharp intake of breath, but before he could stop, her fingers slid into his hair, urging him on. He teased her other nipple, then worked his way downwards, nuzzling her abdomen as he slid one hand between her thighs.

He cupped her sex, feeling how hot and damp she was. She wanted this as much as he did. But he had to be completely sure. 'Sophie. May I touch you?'

'If you don't,' she said, her voice shaky, 'I may have to kill you.'

He slid one finger along her cleft, noting the way she shuddered when he touched the sensitive spot of her clitoris. He did it again, just to be sure. And again and again, until she was shuddering with need and gripping him hard.

'Charlie. Please. Now,' she begged.

'Not yet.' He replaced his hand with his mouth, alternating flicks of his tongue with suction, and Sophie whimpered.

'Charlie, I'm going to…'

The rest of her sentence was lost as he tasted her climax.

She shuddered once, twice, and he shifted up to pull her into his arms.

'Charlie. That was…'

'Just the beginning,' he promised. 'I still have quite a bit of my theory to prove.'

'Wha' theory?' Her voice was slurred with pleasure.

It was good to know he could turn her brain to mush. He'd remember how next time they had an argument.

He rubbed his nose against hers. 'That we can wipe out the past. Start with a clean slate. Just you and me.'

'Uh-huh.'

'So let's try a little erasing.' He rolled onto his back and pulled her on top of him.

She quivered as she realised she was straddling his erection.

'I want you, Sophie,' he said softly. 'But I'm not going to pressure you.'

She tilted her hips. 'This feels like pressure.'

He groaned. 'Uh. OK. I think I'll have to start from ten thousand and count back in multiples of seventy-three.' But he wasn't sure if even that would take his mind off the fact that he really, really, *really* wanted to be inside Sophie. Right now.

'I've got a better idea,' Sophie said, and leaned down to kiss him.

By the time she lifted her head again, Charlie couldn't think straight. And he was almost inside her when he remembered. 'Condom.'

She stopped, and her eyes widened in horror. Clearly she'd

realised just how irresponsible they'd both been about to be. 'I haven't got any.'

Which made this a very delicate situation. 'I, um, have.'

Her eyes narrowed again. 'You came here tonight expecting to make love? Or do you just carry them with you all the time?'

'Neither.' He flushed. 'I'm just…trying to be responsible.' No way could he tell her it was Seb's idea. She'd be horrified at the idea of him discussing something so private. Not that he'd actually discussed it. Seb had just been—well, typical Seb. Seb lived, thought and breathed sex.

'Where is it?'

'My wallet. Trouser pocket.' He took a shuddering breath. 'Sophie…I'm not taking you for granted, I swear. I never will.'

'You'd better not,' she said, and climbed off him.

Please. Please, just let her get the condom. Don't let her stop now. Please, he begged silently.

And then she handed him his wallet.

He shook his head. 'No. This has to be your choice.'

'You trust me with your wallet?'

'I'd trust you,' he said simply, 'with my life. And, for the record, my wallet's virtually empty.'

'Like the Queen—you don't carry cash?'

The sparkle in her eye belied the sharpness of her question. 'No. I gave most of my cash to the cabbie who brought me here. And spent the rest of it on some not-very-special flowers. Which you didn't want anyway.'

'I was…well, angry with you,' she admitted. 'Because I didn't want flowers. I wanted you.'

'You have me,' he reminded her. 'Completely at your mercy.'

'Since you put it that way…' She opened his wallet, took out the condom, unwrapped it and slid it over his penis.

He groaned.

'I didn't hurt you?' Sophie asked, clearly worried.

'No. It's just… I need you to touch me. But it's your decision.'

'I've made my decision,' she said, and straddled him again.

Charlie was almost hyperventilating as she sank down onto him, but he could see the fear in her face. 'You're in control,' he told her shakily. 'You don't have to do anything you don't want to. We can stop whenever you want to stop.' Even though it would leave him burning with frustration.

'I don't want to stop.'

'Make love with me, Sophie,' he tempted her. 'Let me take you to the edge of the universe, where there's nothing but you and me. Let it all go.'

Slowly, hesitatingly, she began to lift and lower herself over him. He supported her hips, just liking the feel of her skin against his. 'With my body,' he whispered, 'I thee worship.'

And, please, God, he'd be saying that to her soon in front of an audience—one of whom would be wearing white robes and carrying a Bible.

He felt her body begin to ripple round him, and then his own climax hit him. Hard.

He wasn't sure how much later it was, but she was lying in his arms. And his skin was wet. She was crying.

He stroked her back. 'Sophie? Are you all right? Did I hurt you?'

'No,' she said, her voice muffled. 'It's just…I think I'm free. After all these years I'm free of the nightmare.' She shifted to support herself on her hands so she could look into his face. 'And it's going to be all right.'

'Better than all right,' he promised her. 'It's just going to get better and better.' He paused. 'I love you, Sophie. I think I've loved you from the moment I first met you.'

'Me, too. Except I was trying to deny it because I...because of the past.'

Say it. Oh, please—just say it, he thought. *Me, too* wasn't enough. He wanted to hear the words.

He waited, beseeching her with his eyes.

And she told him. 'It's a clean slate. I love you.'

The whole world felt as if it were filled with rainbows. All was definitely right with his world. He smiled. 'The more I get to know you, the more I know I want to spend the rest of my life with you. Will you marry me, Sophie?'

'Maybe we should do this without marriage,' she said.

He frowned. 'Cohabit, you mean? We could. But...why?'

'Your family,' she said softly. 'It's going to be hard for them to accept me.'

'Absolutely not. Seb and Vicky sent me here tonight. That's why I didn't have dinner—they told me to stop wasting time and sort things out with you.'

There was a shocked pause. 'Did the press follow you?' she asked.

'Not after Vicky's phone call. I bet they couldn't get to the restaurant fast enough.' He chuckled. 'We have an official date, by the way. Some time soon there's going to be a fundraiser at a certain hospital in Docklands. A promise auction. And a certain Sebastian Radley is the night's star prize.'

She blinked in surprise. 'Your brother's selling himself?'

'In aid of a couple of good causes. Financially for the hospital, and emotionally for us. He also says that we owe him the position of best man.' He raised an eyebrow. 'So, actually, you have to marry me. To save me from being scalped.'

'Is Seb a surgeon?'

Charlie shook his head. 'He's in ED. But Vicky's a neuro-surgeon. And she's with him in this.'

'So I have to marry you.'

'Yes.' He licked his lower lip. 'Though I'm quite happy to do a little…persuading.'

She laughed. 'I see. Sophie Radley. Well, it sounds OK. Mrs Sophie Radley.'

'Um, no, You'll be Lady Radley, actually,' he corrected. 'And our children will all be Honourables.'

She shook her head. 'I am *not* having Lady Radley on my bank account or my hospital pass!'

'You can call yourself Mrs if you like.' He smiled. 'Seb loves being an Honourable, but my bank account's just R. C. Radley.'

'Not Lord?'

'Not Lord. My choice. I'm a doctor first. Though I think being a doctor will take third place.'

She frowned. 'What do you mean?'

'Husband first, father second, doctor third, and baron comes way, way down the list.' He smiled. 'But I'm jumping the gun. I haven't spoken to your father yet.'

She blinked. 'You're going to do it the traditional way?'

'I don't want to get married without your family's blessing. Without your parents knowing that I'll honour you, love you and protect you for the rest of my days.'

'And if my father says no?' she tested.

'Then I'll prove it to him, so he changes his mind.'

'How?'

'I'll think of something,' Charlie said, 'if it happens.'

'Actually,' Sophie said thoughtfully, 'it won't. Because if he says no, my mum might have something to say about it.'

He smiled. 'I think I'm going to like your mum. She makes the best cake in the world *and* she's on my side?' He rubbed his nose against hers. 'Better and better. Are you on duty tomorrow?'

'No.'

'Good. Neither am I.' He kissed her lightly. 'So. Tomorrow morning we go and see your parents. Tomorrow afternoon we go shopping. For an engagement ring. I mean, there *is* an heirloom ring, and you're more than welcome to it, but I want something that's just for you and me. Starting a new tradition.' The beginnings of a new family, one that loved each other. A family where he really belonged.

'No can do. Shopping, I mean. It's one of my family Sundays,' Sophie said.

'OK. We see your parents, we go shopping, and we come back for your family Sunday.' He paused. 'That is, if you think they'd like to celebrate our engagement? We could, um, take champagne for our pot-luck contribution. A case of it. And something nice for the kids.'

Sophie smiled. 'You know, Lord Radley, I think you're going to fit into the Harrison family just fine.'

He smiled back. 'For now—and for always.'

MILLS & BOON®

Live the emotion

_MedicaL
romance™

NEEDED: FULL-TIME FATHER
by Carol Marinelli

The grand opening of Heatherton A&E doesn't quite
go to plan, so nurse manager Madison Walsh must
rely on, and trust, new consultant Guy Boyd to save
the day. Trusting turns to loving, but Madison has
her daughter's happiness to consider...

TELL ME YOU LOVE ME *by Gill Sanderson*

John Cameron is a loner, travelling the world as a
professional diver. For reasons of his own he's wary
of getting close to anyone – until he meets Dr Abbey
Fraser. John instinctively knows he needs to be part
of her life. Then they discover they share a secret...

THE SURGEON'S ENGAGEMENT WISH
by Alison Roberts

Nurse Beth Dawson has chosen small town life for
some peace and quiet. The last person she expects
to meet is Luke Savage, the high-flying surgeon she
was once engaged to! Luke has changed, mellowed
– realised what's important in life. But will he forgive
Beth for leaving him?

*A&E DRAMA: Pulses are racing in these
fast-paced dramatic stories*

On sale 3rd February 2006

*Available at WHSmith, Tesco, ASDA, Borders, Eason,
Sainsbury's and most bookshops*

www.millsandboon.co.uk

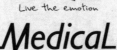

BEFORE SUNRISE
by Diana Palmer

Enter a world of passion, intrigue and heartfelt emotion. As two friends delve deeper into a murder investigation they find themselves entangled in a web of conspiracy, deception...and a love more powerful than anything they've ever known.

THE BAY AT MIDNIGHT
by Diane Chamberlain

Her family's cottage on the New Jersey shore was a place of freedom and innocence for Julie Bauer – until tragedy struck…

Don't miss this special collection of original romance titles by bestselling authors.

4 FREE

BOOKS AND A SURPRISE GIFT!

We would like to take this opportunity to thank you for reading this Mills & Boon® book by offering you the chance to take FOUR more specially selected titles from the Medical Romance™ series absolutely FREE! We're also making this offer to introduce you to the benefits of the Reader Service™—

- ★ **FREE home delivery**
- ★ **FREE gifts and competitions**
- ★ **FREE monthly Newsletter**
- ★ **Exclusive Reader Service offers**
- ★ **Books available before they're in the shops**

Accepting these FREE books and gift places you under no obligation to buy, you may cancel at any time, even after receiving your free shipment. Simply complete your details below and return the entire page to the address below. You don't even need a stamp!

YES! Please send me 4 free Medical Romance books and a surprise gift. I understand that unless you hear from me, I will receive 6 superb new titles every month for just £2.75 each, postage and packing free. I am under no obligation to purchase any books and may cancel my subscription at any time. The free books and gift will be mine to keep in any case.

M6ZED

Ms/Mrs/Miss/Mr ....Initials ....
BLOCK CAPITALS PLEASE

Surname ....

Address ....

....

....Postcode................................

Send this whole page to:
UK: FREEPOST CN81, Croydon, CR9 3WZ

Offer valid in UK only and is not available to current Reader service subscribers to this series. Overseas and Eire please write for details. We reserve the right to refuse an application and applicants must be aged 18 years or over. Only one application per household. Terms and prices subject to change without notice. Offer expires 30th April 2006. As a result of this application, you may receive offers from Harlequin Mills & Boon and other carefully selected companies. If you would prefer not to share in this opportunity please write to The Data Manager, PO Box 676, Richmond, TW9 IWU.

Mills & Boon® is a registered trademark owned by Harlequin Mills & Boon Limited.
Medical Romance™ is being used as a trademark. The Reader Service™ is being used as a trademark.